# BRADLEY

## LOVING A YOUNG SERIES, BOOK 6

## STACY EATON

# CHAPTER ONE

## NOLAN

"*A*re you sure you don't want to look at another house?" my friend Kayley asked hesitantly from behind me.

"No! This one is perfect, Kay!"

I heard a clatter and spun to see her trying to catch the cabinet door before it hit the floor. When she turned to me, clutching it tightly to her chest, her eyes were wide and she was wincing. "Perfect, Nolan? This house is far from perfect. The damn thing should be condemned! I can't believe it's even on the market. The owners should have bulldozed it and sold off the land."

"Ah, come on, Kayley. It needs a little bit of work, that's all. I'm not afraid of getting my hands dirty. You know I like to fix things. That's one of the reasons that you and I became such great friends."

She shook her head and set the cabinet door on the counter. "Girl, there is a huge difference in fixing things on a house you own and buying a house that is ready to fall down around you before you can even move in. Did you ever see the movie about the couple that buys their fixer-upper dream house, and it is nothing but a nightmare, and they practically kill one another?"

1

I laughed. "I guess it's a good thing I'm not married any longer, and this house is not that bad."

She gave me a stern look. "You need an eye test. Let's just talk about the kitchen here for a moment, shall we?" She didn't wait for me to respond as she continued. "Obviously, the cabinets need to be replaced, or at least a heavy sanding, a new coat of paint, and hardware—boy, do they need new hardware, and the counter is warped." She shook her head, talking more to herself as she bent down eye level with the counter. "I don't think I have ever seen a warped countertop like this before."

"Relax. I have every intention of putting in new countertops."

"Yeah, well, you are going to need new appliances, a new floor, and—" She bent over and opened the cabinet under the sink. "Holy crap, all new pipes." She was shaking her head as she stood again. "Seriously, Nolan. We need to walk away from this."

"No. Kayley, you know as well as I do that I can do almost all of this on my own."

She gave me a doubtful look. "When did you get your plumber's license?"

"You are so dramatic."

"And you are stupid if you are even considering this house. We already looked at four other homes that would be perfect for you and the kids that are all move-in ready, and I still have another four to show you. None of them need anywhere the amount of work that this one does."

I shrugged and sighed. "I know. That's why I want this one. It will keep me busy. I'm not going to have the kids for another three months. Having a house to work on will keep me from going nuts without them."

"You are going to be working and coaching. You are already going to be busy. Besides, this isn't a three-month project for one person—it's a *three-year* project for a couple!"

"Pft. Not busy enough. You know that I can't stand sitting around, Kayley. Without the kids, the next few months are going to be a nightmare. I need something that is going to exhaust me every day so that I crash at night and not lie around missing them."

"Then get a hobby or buy one of the other places and repaint every room and plant a garden. That will keep you busy."

I crossed my arms over my chest and studied Kayley. Her reddish-blond hair was shorter than it had been when she lived in New York. It looked nice, and the glow on her face fit her beautifully. I couldn't wait to see her with her stomach poking out as she shuffled around. "You realize that you do exactly what I'm planning on doing every day in your job, right?"

"Yeah, I am aware of that, but I'm a paid professional. Not a schoolteacher that is taking up remodeling as an expensive hobby."

I laughed—hard. "You know, less than a year ago, you were a paid professional selling houses. Now you are helping your brother build them, and you don't even build them now that you are pregnant and everyone told you no."

"Hey, I help when he needs it. Just the other day, I was slinging my hammer and framing a garage."

"Oh, I bet Cam loved that. Why is it weird that I want to fix up my own place when you do it for other people?"

"What Cam thinks is null and void, and it's not weird at all, Nolan. I just think you should start with a house that doesn't need ninety-nine percent of it torn down before you can live in it."

I laughed. I knew Kayley was only looking out for me. She'd been doing that since I called her and told her I was getting divorced. That was two years ago, and she had helped me find a small house that would work for me and my two girls, who were then eight and ten. When Kayley moved away, I'd lost my best friend, tennis partner, and drinking buddy. I'd also been fired from coaching the boys' soccer team and told in no uncertain terms that I should stick to teaching. They said that coaching a boys' team was no place for a woman like me.

A woman like me? What the hell did that mean? Did they mean a competitive, brutally honest, hardworking woman, who expected everyone to do their best and give their all to succeed? If they didn't want my style of coaching, then fine!

So I started to look for a new place to coach. Then, after some upper management positions changed at the middle school where I was employed, I got irritated with my job altogether and decided that moving wasn't such a bad idea.

Kayley's sister, Riley, was a teacher in elementary school here in Millerstown, and she'd heard that they were looking for a couple more teachers at the middle school. When I called, I found they were looking for a new soccer coach, but not just for the boys but also for the girls' team. I told them I'd take on either team. After a couple of visits down here, I had my certification to teach in Pennsylvania, a new job, kids to coach, and now I was shopping for a house.

The hardest part of all of this was that I had left my girls in New York to stay with my parents while I got situated and so they could finish the school year. I had never been away from them for more than a couple of weeks, and I knew that I had to keep myself busy enough that I made it through the next three months.

My ex-husband had tried to fight me on moving, but then I reminded him that he had moved five hundred miles away from the girls to be with his new wife. I also reminded him that I was now closer to him and his previous eight-hour drive was only four. Eventually, he got on board with it, and I think that had a lot to do with his new wife. It was the only thing I appreciated about her. She didn't want him arguing with me because it took time away from their relationship and put him in a bad mood.

I hadn't liked her from the day I met her. Well, I didn't like her before that either. She'd been sleeping with my husband for two years while we were married. I did know that she was pleasant to the kids, and she made sure they had fun and were taken care of when they went to visit—I appreciated that too.

Kayley broke me out of my thoughts. "Nolan, I'm serious here. This place will be too much work and way too expensive."

"It won't be too expensive, Kayley. I can get this house for a steal. You already said that, and I can use that extra money I saved from the sale of my place to put back into the house."

"Saving fifty grand on the purchase price of the house and spending a hundred is not saving money, Nolan."

I sighed. I knew Kayley was probably right, but I wanted this house. The minute I had seen the overgrown front garden and the wraparound porch that begged for some tender loving care, I had fallen in love with it.

I approached Kayley. "I know you want what is best for me, but, Kayley, this is the type of house that I have dreamed of owning since I was a little girl. Once I restore it, it is going to be beautiful—absolutely stunning."

She huffed as she shook her head. "Fine. If this is what you *really* want, I will put an offer on it for you."

Even though Kayley wasn't doing real estate full-time anymore, she had gotten her Pennsylvania license to help friends out once in a while and to keep her toes in the water in case things went terrible working with her brother.

I squealed as I grabbed her hands. "Thank you! How long do you think it will take?"

"Considering the house has been on the market for almost two years, and no one has lived in it or even put an offer in on it the whole time, I'm thinking pretty quickly."

"Great!" I clapped my hands together. "Then let's put an offer in."

She shook her head. "Alright, if you seriously want to."

"Yes! You realize that I'll only be a couple of miles away from you and no longer sleeping in your guest room. I'm sure that Cam will appreciate it." I winked at her, and she finally smiled.

"Oh, I'm sure Cam would appreciate one less person in the house for a little while, but you know you are welcome to stay as long as you need to. I don't think you will be living here for a while."

"No! I'm going to move in as soon as I own it. The best way to work on it is to immerse myself into the project completely."

Kayley glanced around, her eyes skimming over the cobwebs and dirt. I really wasn't blind. I did know that this would be a considerable undertaking, but I was excited to do something for the first time in a long time.

"Nolan, I swear, if I didn't know you better, I'd think you had lost your mind."

I grinned at her and bumped her shoulder. "But you do know me, and you know that my mind was lost a long time ago."

She snickered as she shook her head. "Okay, then why don't we go back to my place, and I'll put an offer in on the house. Just in case some other crazy person is thinking of doing it too."

I laughed. "Yeah, right. Before we go, I want to make a list of the things that I will need to start, like trash bags and brooms and cleaners and things like that."

"You might want to think about a bulldozer instead."

I laughed at her and pulled her arm as I left the kitchen. "Let's start in the bedrooms. Those will be easier."

It was three hours later before we left, and I carried with me a list of projects that would need my attention. The list was over two pages long. Then I had a list of tools and supplies that I would need, which was another three pages. Luckily, Kayley said that some of the tools I could borrow, like the saws and such. Her brother had quite a few older tools that she knew he'd let me use.

With that decided, we left the house and went back to hers

to put in the offer. I did not doubt that they would accept it, especially after having it on the market with no traffic for two years.

I made us lunch while she worked at the kitchen table, and before she sent it over, she called the agent who had listed it.

"Hello, Marianne. It's Kayley Young. How are you?"

I listened to the one-sided conversation, gnawing on my bottom lip so hard, I was surprised I didn't peel the skin off. Kayley told her that she had a buyer for the property, told her what I was willing to offer, which was twenty thousand less than I had told her to offer—but Kayley insisted. There were a lot of 'yeps,' 'I know,' and 'I did,' said in that conversation from Kayley's side.

Finally, Kayley said, "Okay, I'm emailing it over to you right now. I'll look forward to hearing from you."

When she hung up, I stared at her wide-eyed. "Well?"

"Well, she wanted to make sure you knew that the house is being sold as-is, and there is no warranty on this house at all. The owners are not willing to negotiate on repairs, so when the house inspection goes through, you can't ask them to fix *anything*."

"I know. I already told you that I was good with that."

"Yeah, I told Marianne that."

"So, what happens now?"

She clicked a few things on her computer and then pushed it away. "Now we wait for the homeowner to either accept or come back with another number."

"What do you think they are going to do?"

She laughed loudly. "I think they are going to take your money and laugh all the way to the bank."

# CHAPTER TWO

## BRADLEY

*I* was hanging a sheet of drywall when I heard a car pull down the driveway of my worksite. My father was either coming to check on me, or my mother was making sure that I had eaten lunch. You would think by now that they would know I could take care of the business and myself.

It didn't matter that I was forty. My mother still made sure I ate properly and always seemed to have an extra sandwich in a cooler in her car just in case. She told me that she carried that because you never know who might need a meal. I was pretty sure she checked up on Henley and Hunt too.

My father was retired, but that didn't stop him from overseeing the jobs I did. It hadn't always been that way, but ever since my wife had passed several years ago from cancer, they had put it upon themselves to make sure that I kept going.

For a time after Cheryl died, I'd had issues getting out of bed and going to work. Eating was never something I thought about either, but what did keep me going were my children, Tonya and Tyler.

It was for them that I got out of bed every morning, showered, dressed, and made breakfast. Because of the kids, I went to work every day and made sure I was home at night to feed them dinner and help with homework.

There wasn't a day that I didn't think about Cheryl in some fashion. Now, it didn't hurt as much, and I'd gotten over the loss. Getting out of bed was a habit now, just like eating and doing everything else in life—except dating.

I needed everyone in my family to get off my back about that. I'd be alright, and when the time was right, I would find someone. It wasn't that I hadn't dated; I'd gone out on a couple of dates over the last two years, but I'd gotten irritated by how the women kept referring to me as a widower and how they went on and on about how sad it must be to raise two children on my own.

Yeah, it was sad, but the kids and I were okay. Plus, I had a lot of help. Especially now that all my siblings were in solid relationships and having children of their own. Charlotte and Wes were the last ones to bring a new member to the family only last month with their son, Michael. Kayley and Cameron were adding to the expanding Young family, and one day, Roxanne and Henley would join the kids' club. There was always someone around to help get Tonya or Tyler to the doctor or sports.

With Tonya being twelve now and Tyler ten, they had active social lives, and they were always on the go. Thank god for cellphones, or I wouldn't know where they were or who they were with.

"Hey, you have all the drywall up." Kayley's voice surprised me, and I glanced back as I pulled the drill from the last screw that I was about to put in.

"I didn't expect you here today. I thought you were showing your friend houses."

"I did. I showed her several, and she got stuck on one, so we didn't see the rest." She scanned the area. "She put an offer in already."

"Really? That's great," I told Kayley as I turned back to my work and drilled the last drywall screw into place.

"Well, it is great, but—" She paused, and I turned to her.

"But what?"

"She put an offer in on the old Millstone house."

I laughed. "Why the hell would she do that? That place is a wreck. The only person that should buy that is someone who wants the property. It needs a complete demolition."

"That's what I told her, but she is hell-bent on restoring it."

"Kayley." I studied her. "Please tell me you tried to talk her out of it."

"Ha! I tried, trust me, but you haven't met her, Brad. There is no talking her out of anything." She paused. "I did want to know if you—"

Oh, here it comes. I put my hand up to stop her. "Don't even ask me to help your friend. The last thing I will do is help a woman who thinks she can take on a tremendous job like that and then realizes she made a huge mistake."

She slammed her fists to her hips. "That's not what I was going to ask. Besides, if she batted her pretty brown eyes at you, you'd be begging her to let you help."

I laughed. "I doubt that." Kayley was quiet for a moment, too quiet. I glanced back to see her eyeing me up. "What?"

"Actually, you might like her."

"No! Just no!" I growled. "I'm sick and tired of you all trying to set me up with your friends. I am quite happy on my own, thank you." I went to grab the spackle so that I could start covering the seams and nail holes.

"Whatever, Brad. You know that one of these days, you're going to meet someone and finally let yourself fall in love again. Cheryl is probably pacing around heaven pissed that you are still single and walking around with your tail between your legs."

"I am not walking around with my tail between my legs,

Kay." I shook my head at her. "I have a busy life, and I'm not interested in dating right now."

"Are you interested in sex?"

I turned away from her. Oh, sex I would be interested in having. It had been so long I could join a monastery. "No," I lied.

"Liar!" She laughed. "I don't know any man who doesn't want to have sex."

"Yeah, well, you know someone now," I muttered.

Kayley sighed. "Brad, I get that you miss Cheryl, but you gotta let that go. You know that she would want you to be happy. She would want you to find someone to love again."

I ignored Kayley as I prepared to slather on the spackle.

Kayley came around to my side so she could see my face. "Would it be so bad to be in a relationship?"

"Kay, I will admit that the thought of having sex is nice, but I don't want to deal with all those women who talk about how hard it might be for me to take care of my children or how they feel so sorry for me because my wife died."

"Then stop acting sorry for yourself, Bradley. They wouldn't do that if you didn't walk around all mopey and sad."

"I am not mopey," I replied gruffly.

"Yes, you are. Sometimes I think you are that way so that people stay away from you, but it's time to stop being a baby and get back out there. I did."

I laughed. "Yeah, you are so not me, Kay."

"No, I'm not, but I'm your sister, and I love you. If I can find someone to love *me*, then you can find someone to love *you*."

"It's not that simple."

"It's never simple."

"I have kids to think about and a business."

"Do you think that women your age don't have lives, careers, or baggage that they have to deal with? Wake up, Bradley. You are not the only one with issues. You're forty. Do you want to spend the next thirty years alone?"

I didn't respond, and I heard my sister sigh wearily. "I wasn't going to try and set you up with her or ask you to help her. I was merely going to ask if I could loan her a few tools so that she doesn't have to buy them all."

I glanced at her; brow raised. "She's going to do it herself?"

"Yep, if you thought I was a tomboy, you should see Nolan. She puts me to shame."

"Nolan?"

"Yes."

I frowned. "Nolan is a girl?"

Kayley laughed with a shrug. "Yes, and yes, it is an odd name for a girl, but her father wanted a boy."

I shook my head. Why would anyone name a girl Nolan?

"Well, do you mind if I loan her a few things?"

"Yeah, you can loan her some of my tools, but I am not going to take responsibility if she hurts herself with them, and I am not going to go over and bail her out when she gets in over her head—so don't ask."

Kayley put her hands up. "I won't. I'll help her with what she needs."

I stared at her stomach, then lifted my eyes to her. "You shouldn't be doing that in your condition."

"Don't you start too! I know damn well what I can and can't do."

I huffed. "You going to have time to help her?"

"I'll do it at night and on the weekends. She's going to be working during the day too, so that's the only time she'll have."

"Aw, okay. Just don't overdo it. You need to stay unstressed and get plenty of rest."

"Yes, dear," she snapped as her cellphone rang. "Excuse me. I have to take this."

She stepped off to the side, and I focused on what I was doing. I had a bad feeling about her friend taking on a project that big. Just like when Daniella's house had burned down, and

13

my father had handed over my services to her without my approval. I was going to get wrapped up in having to help with Kayley's friend too. Damn it. That was the last thing that I needed right now, especially if my sister decided to play matchmaker.

"Wow, okay, well, I'll let her know. Thank you, Marianne."

When Kayley hung up, I turned to her. "Whatever that was, it sounded good."

"Nolan got the house. They even went five thousand under what she offered to give her extra money to work on the house."

"Man, they *really* wanted to get rid of that property, didn't they?"

"Yeah." She shook her head. "And I *really* did try to talk her out of it. This house is going to be a nightmare, but she's determined."

"Well, good luck to her."

"She's gone through a few tough years. She deserves happiness. The only reason I did put the offer in for her was that this is the first time that I've seen her excited about something in a long time."

"Good for her." I wasn't interested in her friend's personal life, but I didn't want to be rude to my sister.

Kayley looked around. "Do you need my help?"

"Nah, I got this. I'm just going to spackle the walls and then head out. I have to pick up Tonya, and these walls need to dry. I'll sand them in the morning."

"Alright, well, I'll be here bright and early. Think we can get the primer up on the walls tomorrow?"

"Yeah, we should be able to. If we both sand and get the second coat of spackle on, we can work on the trim while it dries, then get the primer up. They still haven't decided if they want me to paint it an actual color. I told them that most people didn't, but the wife keeps thinking it needs to be a color."

Kayley chuckled. "Women, right? Okay, sounds good. I'll see you tomorrow."

"Yep, see you tomorrow, and tell your friend congrats on the house."

Kayley started walking backward. "I will. You really should meet her. Now that I think about it, you two would be the perfect couple."

"Go away, Kayley. There is no such thing as a perfect couple."

"Ha! Look around you, Brad. Your entire family is full of perfect couples."

I waved over my shoulder to let her know I heard her, and I was done with the conversation. I didn't want to admit it to her, but she was right. My parents had been married for forty-two years, and over the last two years, my five siblings had all found someone to love and spend their life with.

I didn't want to be alone for the rest of my life, but I also wasn't ready to settle for someone who wasn't perfect for me. I needed someone who would readily accept my children but not try to take over as their mom. I wanted a woman who didn't expect me to make a million dollars and who would be happy eating leftovers at home instead of going out for a fancy dinner.

I spread the spackle as I continued to think about the perfect woman for me. She'd like to get her hands dirty, maybe help me once in a while, but still be able to slip on a dress and heels and be feminine.

Speaking of femininity, I pursed my lips as I thought of Kayley's friend, Nolan. I shook my head. Seriously, how could anyone name a baby girl Nolan? That was about as unfeminine as you could get.

# CHAPTER THREE

## NOLAN

our weeks later, the papers were signed, and I had the keys in hand. As I climbed the rickety front steps to the porch, I was grinning as if I'd just won the lottery.

Even as we went to the table to sign the papers this morning, Kayley had been actively trying to talk me out of this house, but I was determined. Every night for the last two weeks, I had dreamed of the place. I would admit that a few of those dreams had been little nightmares, but I'd only admit that to myself.

It was *my* house, and I was sticking by it. I could not wait to begin tomorrow. Even though I had just started my new job, I'd taken Wednesday through Friday off to be here for the delivery from the home store and start working on my place.

I had it all planned out. For the first week and a half, I would remain at Kayley's house and come here each night after work or coaching to clean. My priority was to clean the master bedroom and get the bathroom useable. It shouldn't take me more than a week to get those two rooms cleaned, painted, and ready to use. Next weekend, I could move in and begin working on the kitchen.

I let myself into the house, giggling as I bounced on my toes, but then I felt the wood under my feet give a little bit, and I jumped off the porch and into the foyer of the house. The porch would need to be replaced soon, or someone would get hurt walking into the house.

In the foyer, I stood, my heart filling with excitement as I stared up at the grand chandelier. It had seen better days—much better days. I wondered if I'd be able to find replacement crystals for that. There had to be someone out there that made and sold those. I'd have to add that to my list to search for replacements.

I headed toward the kitchen, grinning the whole way until I heard something scuttle along the floor. I paused and listened. It was probably a mouse. I had already purchased mousetraps because mice were bound to move in when a house was unoccupied. I reached the threshold of the kitchen and peered in but didn't see anything.

The little critters were more scared of me than I was of them. It wouldn't be long before they realized that I was the new owner, and they were being evicted.

I grinned as I stood in the kitchen and looked around. I could imagine this room with clean windows, new curtains, and all-new cupboards and counters. It was going to look amazing. I scuffed my foot along the wood floor. Wow, that was a lot of caked-on dirt. It would take a lot of hard work to redo these floors, but they would look amazing once they were finished.

I walked from room to room, picturing in my mind what it would look like completed. Maybe I was crazy for taking on this project, but I knew I could do it. I might need help once in a while, but that was okay. I didn't have an aversion to hiring someone to do certain things, like plumbing and electricity. I could fix *things*, but water and electricity were not things I wanted to mess around with.

I continued through the house and stood in the master

bedroom, staring at the windows. Once I washed the panes of glass and added new window treatments, it would change the entire room. The floor here wasn't quite as bad as the central part of the house, and I was excited about that. I pulled open the door to the closet, and the handle fell off in my hands. "Whoops!" I messed with it for a few moments, trying to put it back on, but it wasn't going to stay. I set it aside on the floor and mentally made a note to add another one to the list. Maybe I should change all the doorknobs in the room.

Inside the closet, I grinned. It was huge for an older home, almost the size of a small bedroom, and I was thrilled to be able to design shelves for it and give myself a fancy dressing room of sorts—all this space and no one to share it with. I giggled as I danced in a circle. I had it all to myself.

I made my way into the bathroom and stared at the shower. Where the closet was large, the bathroom was tiny. I pushed on a few ceramic tiles on the back of the shower wall, and they shifted—of course. The wallboard behind them seemed soft. I'd have to replace it eventually, but hopefully not at first. I took in the showerhead and shivered. Good thing I had already bought a new one of those. The relic hanging there was no doubt filled with rust.

I stood back and surveyed the bathroom. I could make the shower a little bigger. It might make the bathroom smaller, but it was possible. If I removed the cast iron tub, I could make it a walk-in shower. That would make the room seem more open. I wasn't one to soak in tubs anyway, so I wouldn't miss that.

I would need the plumber to tell me if the pipes were in good order. I could figure out the best kind of shower to install after he did. Good thing I had already called one, and he was going to come first thing tomorrow to look over the pipes in the kitchen and three bathrooms to give me a quote on what was needed.

I might have called three plumbers back in New York to

make sure I got a fair estimate, but Kayley told me I could trust this guy.

The house had five bedrooms upstairs and two full baths. Downstairs, it had a traditional living and dining room and a large eat-in kitchen with a half bath and laundry room next to the family room at the rear of the house. It didn't have a garage, but that was okay. I had land on the property to have one built —but that was a project for the future.

As I looked around, I realized that I did have a lot to keep me busy, and I tried not to let it overwhelm me. The patching and painting alone would take a while.

There was a knock at the door, and then I heard it open. The squeak was undeniable. Add a spray can of lubricant to my list, check!

"Hello!" Kayley called out, and I went down to meet her.

"Hey, I thought you were busy this afternoon," I told her as I came down into the foyer.

"Brad found someone to help him, so he didn't need me after all. Besides, what kind of a friend would I be if I wasn't here to help you on your first day?"

I hugged her tightly. "You're the best, Kayley." I stepped back and studied her. "Really, you are the best. I'm not sure where I would be right now if it weren't for you."

"I'm going to accept that compliment quickly because I have a feeling in a couple of days, once you start tearing into this house, you're going to change your mind."

"Change my mind?"

"Yeah, you're going to hate me for not talking you out of this house."

I laughed. "Never!"

"We'll see." She held up a large gift bag. "A little gift for you."

I took the bag, and we headed into the kitchen. "A little gift? This bag is huge! You didn't have to do this, you know."

"I know, but I wanted to." I stuck my hand into the bag, but she stopped me. "Wait, there is an order to this."

"Then why did you give it to me?" I laughed as I handed it back to her. She reached in and removed a loaf of French bread. I frowned.

"Bread, so you may never go hungry." I grinned as she stuck her hand back in and pulled out a bottle of olive oil. "May you always have health and well-being, plus it's great to dip your bread in."

I chuckled as she went back for more and removed a bottle of fancy pink salt and a candle. "Salt so you will always have flavor in your life, plus you can sprinkle it on slugs to kill them if you find any around the house."

"Gross."

"Here is a candle so that you will always have light."

"Holy cow, how much do you have in there?" I asked as she dug for more.

She pulled out a pineapple, and I laughed. "May your home always be welcoming and blessed by friendship."

"Aw."

"Two more things." She smiled my way as she handed the pineapple over and then pulled out a bottle of sparkling grape juice. "May you always have a reason to toast, and the last thing is in my pocket." She pulled it out and handed me a dollar bill. "May you never be broke."

"Oh, my god! Kayley. This is so cute! Thank you so much! That dollar might come in handy," I told her as I set the pineapple beside the nonalcoholic wine and hugged her tightly again. "I have a feeling I'm going to need every spare dollar I can get!"

"I almost gave you a hundred-dollar bill," she said around a chuckle. "Because one dollar isn't going to get you much for this house, but it's the thought that counts."

"I appreciate it." I glanced around. "I wish I had a few cups. We could open this bottle and toast to my new house."

"I have cups in the car," she said as she thumbed over her shoulder. "I also have some snacks. I saw that your car was still full of stuff. We can bring all of it in at once."

"Fantastic. Why don't we do that now?"

"No time like the present," she remarked, and we headed out to lug in all the cleaning supplies, tools, and other things that I had brought with me. Of course, I only let her carry the light items, despite her protests.

We were just getting situated to start cleaning when there was another knock on the door, and a man's voice reached us from the foyer.

"Kayley, Nolan? You guys still alive in here?"

Kayley and I laughed as we recognized Cam's voice.

"We're still alive," I called out to him from the kitchen. He came around the corner grinning.

"I wasn't sure if the ghost would have gotten you yet or not."

"Ghost?" A shiver ran down my spine.

"Cam, don't scare her like that. There are no ghosts. That's an old wives' tale."

"Wait! There is an old wives' tale about a ghost?"

Cameron and Kayley shared a glance, like whoops! Kayley turned to me. "There is no such thing as ghosts, Nolan."

"But there is an old wives' tale about ghosts? Like as in haunting this house?"

"Um, yeah," Kayley said but waved it off. "It's no big deal. It's something that kids joke about."

"Did someone die in this house?" I asked quickly.

"Um, not that I know of," Cam replied with a shrug, but Kayley looked a little uncomfortable as she studied the house.

"Kayley? Answer the question."

"No one was killed or anything," she replied.

"Yeah, but did someone die here?"

"I'm pretty sure someone died in this house. It's over a hundred years old." Kayley approached me. "Nolan, it's not haunted."

I studied her, wondering if I could believe her or not. "It better not be haunted. I can take just about anything, but I don't do ghosts."

Kayley laughed. "You mean, all I had to do was tell you the house was haunted, and you wouldn't have bought it?"

"Yes! I told you, I don't do ghosts."

Cam stiffened and then began to step slowly back. Man, he better not be trying to freak me out! I was already freaking.

"Um, ladies." His voice was soft and deep.

"Come on, Cameron. That's not funny," I hissed at him and then turned to Kayley. "Explain what you were talking about."

"No, I'm not playing any games with you," Cameron said softly.

"It's no big deal, Nolan. It's just a story."

"Ladies!" Cam said louder, his eyes trained behind me.

Kayley glanced at him and then around me. She squealed and grabbed my arm. "Don't look behind you."

"Kayley Young! If you even think to tell me that there is a ghost behind me, I'm going to smack you silly."

She shook her head and took a step back, pulling me with her. She kept shaking her head. "No ghost, but how do you feel about snakes?"

"Snakes?"

# CHAPTER FOUR

## BRADLEY

*T*oday, my entire crew was working on a new house. That was my favorite kind of job. I loved when I had a clean slate and a set of blueprints in my hands to work with. I enjoyed doing remodels too, but when I had the chance to build from the ground up, I was thrilled, and so was my entire crew. I also enjoyed doing restorations, but those jobs were few and far between because they were costly.

Chester was my foundation man and always made sure that the concrete pours went smoothly. He also loved masonry, and when I had a fireplace or a stone wall, he was in his element.

Pete was my electrician. He did other things, but he was one hundred percent focused on making sure that the wires and circuits were correct. He was also up to date on the most recent changes in home electronics and appliances. His hope was to one day live in a smart-house entirely controlled by his voice— give me switches and knobs over computers any day.

Milton preferred to put his attention on the bathrooms. His father was a plumber, and while Milton could do anything with a pipe, he excelled at doing tilework and designing incredible bathrooms.

Chad could do just about anything. He was my apprentice and a jack of all trades. He knew the basics of what each of the other men did and assisted them when they needed it. He was also the fastest framer I knew. I swear, if you turned your back, the wall would go up on its own. He also did some remarkable carpentry work for my customers, and he was the only other full-time employee besides myself and my sister.

Milton and I talked as we did an inventory of the materials delivered for the house's framing.

"Yeah, so my father was over at the old Millstone house yesterday."

I smirked at him. "How bad are the pipes?"

"Man, almost every single pipe in the house needs to be replaced. The place has been stagnant for over two years. A lot of the pipes are rusted through and through. It's a good thing the water has been off all that time. Otherwise, it would have flooded itself out. If the homeowner tried to use the pipes now, they would spring leaks like a sprinkler system."

"How much is that going to cost her?"

He glanced at me. "How do you know it's a she?"

"My sister showed her the house."

"Damn, your sister got something against the woman?"

I laughed. "Actually, they are friends from New York, where Kayley used to live."

"You sure they are friends?"

I nodded.

He shook his head. "I'm not sure I would have shown my enemy that house. You met her yet—the new homeowner?"

"No."

"Dad said she's cute as a button but stupid as a brick for buying the property. Said a single woman should never have tried to take on that kind of a project."

"I hope he didn't call her cute as a button to her face."

Milton laughed. "Knowing my dad, he probably did."

I chuckled. "I bet he did. My sister said she's handy."

"Handy or not, she's going to need help. You been over to see the house?"

I shook my head. "Nope, and I told my sister that I was not going to get roped into helping her friend."

"Yeah, right. You're a big softy. She told my dad that she is redoing the entire house. Sounds like a good project to help with and right up your alley. Weren't you just saying the other day how you'd love to do some restoration work?"

I stared at the pile of two-by-fours. "I'm pretty sure I have enough work to do right now."

"Yeah, but this house won't take all that long."

"Long enough for her to hopefully hire someone else."

He chuckled. "Why are you so set against helping her?"

"Because I'm tired of people volunteering my services. My siblings are forever saying, 'Oh, yeah, my brother will help you with that,' and not mentioning that I will charge to do it. I'm not running a free service here. I do have bills to pay."

"I get it. I know a lot of people are forever trying to talk me into designing their dream bathroom, and then I tell them my fees, and they are like, hmm, maybe later."

"Glad to hear that I'm not alone."

"Did you know the lady's name is Nolan? The woman who bought the Millstone place that is."

"Yeah, Kayley told me that."

"What a weird name for a girl." He shook his head. "But my dad did tell her that I designed custom bathrooms, and I know she wanted to redo the master. It's in serious need of repair. The wallboard is molded behind the old tile, so the whole thing needs to come out before she can even think to use it."

"Think she will call you?"

"I hope so. I'd love to do a custom bathroom in a house like that."

"Then maybe she will contact you."

"As long as she calls me after the snake problem is over."

I turned and lifted a brow toward him. "Snake problem?"

"Oh, yeah, I think my dad told her to call Bobby Lee to get them out of her house, plus you know she's got mice, probably bats in the attic, too."

"Wasn't there a rumor that the place was haunted?"

He smirked. "I'd take a ghost over a snake any day."

I chuckled. "Yeah, I probably would too."

Our conversation turned to other things, and it was later that day when Kayley showed up on the site. She stood in the front yard watching Chad work, a smile of satisfaction on her lips that I hoped was for the job he was doing and not the way he looked. She already had one younger man in her life. She sure didn't need two.

"What brings you here today? I thought you were working on the books and doing two estimates."

"All of that is done." She smiled. "I came by here to speak with Milton for a moment. His father told Nolan that he does custom bathrooms. She'd like to see what he can do for her."

"I heard there were snakes in the house."

She shivered. "Oh, yeah, there are. We had an eastern milk snake make itself known. I know they aren't poisonous, but they are scary-looking. Bobby Lee was supposed to search the property and go under the house in the crawl space to see if he found any other critters and seal any holes he finds. I think he's over there now."

Her phone rang, and she held it up as she answered. "Speak of the devil. I was just talking about you."

I heard her loud voice. "Bats! There are bats in my house!"

Kayley chuckled as she looked at me. "How many bats are in your house?"

I laughed as Kayley listened. I could just barely make out the animated voice on the other end of the line. "You know, Kayley, I can handle a lot. I can do a lot, and I knew that the house would have mice and spiders and those other creepy-crawly things, but I never considered snakes and bats living in my house!"

I couldn't help it, but I found myself laughing more as Kayley tried to calm her friend down. "Nolan, no one lived there for two years. It's their house too. You are going to have to make sure they know they are not welcome."

"I know, but come on! Next, I'll find a bear in the closet or something."

Kayley chortled. "I think you are safe on that."

Chad called me over to his side to ask a couple of questions about the blueprints, and when I was done assisting him, Kayley joined us.

"Has she decided that she made a mistake in buying that house yet?"

Kayley chuckled. "Oh, no. She's even more determined than before to restore it to its original beauty."

"Really?"

She nodded. "Although she was a little freaked out when Cam mentioned that the house might be haunted, but that was also when we found the snake in the house."

"Most women I know would have burned the house down once they saw the snake," Chad said with a smirk.

Kayley laughed for a moment. "I would be one of those women, but she's different. She's not your typical woman. Yeah, she's not a fan of snakes and ghosts, but she wasn't screaming and running away."

"Sounds like a rare kind of woman," I commented.

"She is, and that leads me to my next question—"

"No." I sighed. "Before you even ask, the answer is no."

"You don't know the question, Bradley."

"I don't have to to know the answer. You start talking up your friend and then say you have to ask me a question. I am not going out to meet her or ask her out on a date."

Kayley gave me an annoyed look. "That is *not* what I was going to ask."

"Then no, I am not going to help her fix her house."

"Not the question either."

I blew out a frustrated breath and turned to her. "Then tell me the question so I can say no to it correctly."

"When did you turn into such a grump?"

"When you started talking about a woman you think I might be interested in. I'm not, so whatever matchmaking you are doing, it's not going to work."

"Fine, I was wrong. Nolan wouldn't be your type anyway. She's already been married to an asshole; she doesn't need another one in her life."

"Funny. What were you going to ask me?"

"Nolan is thinking of knocking a wall down to open up her kitchen a little bit, but we aren't sure if it's load-bearing. The walls are odd in that house, so I'm not sure either. I was just wondering if you could come over and look at the walls and helps us figure out which ones are load-bearing and which ones aren't."

That shouldn't be a hard thing to do.

"I swear, we are not asking for your help, just your advice."

"When?"

"When you are available."

I glanced at my watch. "I could probably stop by there in about an hour. Would that work?"

"Yep. I'm going to head over there now. She's at work for a little while, but I can show you things before she gets there. Maybe if you're lucky, you won't even have to meet her." Kayley turned and threw a smile over her shoulder.

"I never said that I didn't want to meet your friend, Kay. I said I didn't want to be hooked up with her."

She turned and walked backward. "And I never said I was

going to hook you up, Brad. I just said you might be interested in her."

I shook my head as I turned back to my work. So maybe I was a little bit interested in meeting Nolan. Not because I wanted to get to know her, but Kayley did speak highly of her, and after hearing she was going to do a lot of the work herself, I was curious. Kayley had said she was a tomboy, and with a name like Nolan, I had a distinctive picture of her in my mind. I wondered how close I was.

An hour later, I was standing in the kitchen of the old farmhouse. I had to admit that it did have a lot of potential, but it also had a to-do list two miles long. Man, if I had the time and the money, I'd love to have a project like this to work on myself.

Kayley was on the phone in the family room as I looked around, and I heard the front door open and fast footfalls heading toward the kitchen.

"Would you freaking believe that one of the kids barfed on me today." I turned and opened my mouth to say hello but went speechless as a petite woman came through the threshold with her shirt around her head. She was whipping it off, and it wasn't until she had tossed it on the floor that she looked up and froze.

I didn't want to admire—um, look—but it had been kind of hard not to when all I saw was her trim waist and gray sports bra. My gaze finally made it to her face, and we stared at one another. Her brown eyes were wide as she crossed her arms over her chest, not to hide but to look sterner. "Who are you?"

I found it odd that she didn't seem concerned that she was half naked in front of a stranger. "I'm Kayley's brother, Brad."

"Oh!" She grinned and relaxed her guarded stance. "It's great to meet you." She stepped forward and shoved out her hand.

"It's nice to meet you too." Damn, she was nothing like what I had pictured.

"Nolan, why are you standing there in your sports bra?"

She looked down as if she had forgotten entirely. "Whoops,

sorry, forgot. I got a little distracted when I saw your cute brother in my kitchen. How come you didn't tell me he was so handsome?"

"Because he's my brother," she replied dryly. "Why don't you go put on a shirt before you scare him away."

She laughed, and the sound was so musical that I almost stepped toward her to tell her to do it more. Before I could say anything, she dashed out of the room. My sister reached over and put her hand under my chin.

"You can close your mouth now, Bradley. She isn't your type, and you aren't interested, remember?" She chuckled as she stepped away.

# CHAPTER FIVE

## NOLAN

*S*nakes. My house had bright-red-striped snakes! And bats! Bobby Lee called me and said he thinks he got rid of all three snakes—*three*—and closed up the half dozen holes under the house where they were getting in. He also set down more traps for mice and sprayed around the house and outside for other crawling pests.

In the attic, he found a roost of bats, and that was a different matter. He said it was going to take a little while for those to be taken care of. We couldn't just kill them, and even though they were creepy, I didn't want to kill them anyway. We needed bats in our world.

Bobby Lee suggested a particular device installed at the entrance that would allow them to exit, but it would force them through a tube and back outside when they tried to reenter. Eventually, they would get tired of trying and fly off to find another home. Once they were gone, the entrances would be sealed, and then cleanup would begin.

Bobby Lee made sure to let me know that the cleanup was critical and had to be done by specialists. He had a friend he could call for that, and I asked him to do what needed to be done and take care of it. That extra five grand the sellers had given me was quickly being eaten up by critter control, but that was okay.

What wasn't okay was the seventh grader who decided to eat four cupcakes and a soda before soccer practice and, after doing jumping jacks, hurled all over my shirt and my shoes. The odor made me gag several times as I tried to remain focused on the other players. While I had taken off work, I was still going in for soccer practice in the afternoon.

I was ripping my shirt off as I rushed into the house. I knew Kayley wouldn't be offended. She had seen me in less, and I didn't have much modesty these days. After having kids, the idea of modesty was kind of ludicrous.

What I didn't expect was a sexy man standing in my kitchen eyeing me from head to toe. Well, hello. Before I could enjoy him, I needed to know who he was. I should have realized that this was Kayley's older brother. Now that she had said that, he did seem familiar. I was sure I had seen pictures of him with her before.

I rushed out of the room to grab a new shirt from my plastic container upstairs and then came back down. Brad kept his focus on the walls and off of me as he spoke to Kayley about which one could come down and what needed to stay in place. While he did that, I studied his features. He was a lot taller than me, but that wasn't hard. I was only five foot one. He was in decent shape, but he did physical labor all day, so I wasn't surprised. I kind of loved his beard, too. It wasn't too long, and it wasn't so short that it just looked like scruff.

I zeroed in on the lines around his eyes. I loved a man with laugh lines, but at the same time, I took in the deep furrows of his brow. I needed a man in my life who laughed a lot, but I wasn't sure I wanted one that frowned as often.

He glanced my way, smiling slightly, and I noted that his brown eyes were very similar to mine. I kind of loved that.

Some people thought brown eyes were dull, but there were so many shades that I could find nothing boring about them.

We stared at each other for a moment, and then he seemed to pull his gaze away like he didn't want to but knew he had to. Was that because his sister was in the room with us?

I finally stopped gawking at him and paid attention to what he was saying. The wall that I had initially wanted to remove was a supporting wall, so that was a no-go. Damn. I studied the layout of the kitchen and the walls in regard to the family room. If I shifted all the cabinets to the opposite walls, I could remove that wall and open it up to the family room.

"What about that wall? Could I remove that one?" I pointed to the opposite side of the room.

"You could, but you'd lose all that wall space for cabinets," he replied.

"Not if I flipped the kitchen in the other direction and moved the eat-in part over there near the family room."

He was quiet for a moment as his eyes skimmed the room, and I could imagine him doing calculations in his mind to see if it would fit. I had already done them myself, and I should have a few more inches to play with.

"That would work. It would give you a little more room too."

"I know." I grinned at him as he turned my way again. It took a second, but then he returned the smile.

"That's actually a good idea. That wall could come down, and you would open that area up quite a bit. You could also open up the family room if you changed out that door over there and made it either—"

"A sliding door or French doors?"

"Yeah," he said huskily.

"I already have a set of French doors on my list to add to that room, but I might put a slider. It depends on what I do to the back porch."

"Can I see it, the back porch?"

"Sure," I told him, and he followed me to the back door. As I held it for him, I glanced back at Kayley, who was grinning as if she'd just won the lottery. "You coming?"

"I have to make a phone call." She removed her cellphone from her pocket, and I rolled my eyes. No, she didn't. She was just giving me time to spend with her brother.

On the back deck, Brad was looking over things, and I went down the back steps, calling over my shoulder, "Don't step on the second one down. It's about to break."

"Thanks for the heads-up," he commented.

"I couldn't have you coming over here for some advice and getting hurt. My insurance agent could drop me in a heartbeat since I just started my policy."

He chuckled, and the sound warmed my soul. It had been a long time since a man could glance at me, speak, or laugh, and my entire body would immediately respond.

I wasn't sure what to think of that and realized that I needed to focus on the house and not on Brad. I was about to explain what I was thinking for the porch when I glanced at him and saw him staring out over my property. I had two acres, and it backed up to a hearty line of trees to divide the property from my rear neighbors.

"You have a great yard."

"And a lot to mow," I commented. "If you know anyone selling a good lawn tractor, let me know."

He glanced my way. "I'll keep my eye out. You like mowing?"

I shook my head. "No, I hate it."

"I know a couple of younger guys who do lawn work. Won't cost you an arm and a leg either. They do it to pay for college."

"That would be helpful until I get all the rest of this under control."

"You have any plans for the property?"

"Other than a garage? No, not yet. Although I'd love to make it comfy for friends to gather around, maybe add a firepit."

He grew thoughtful. "You like to swing?"

I chuckled. "Who doesn't like to swing?"

He grinned as he pulled out his phone and messed with it for a moment. "You have such a large backyard area that you should think about doing something like this. Of course, you don't need as many swings, but it's an idea."

He flipped his phone around, and I stared at the image on his screen. "Oh, my god! I love that, Brad. That is so cool." I laughed. "You just happened to have that on your phone?"

He smirked. "Actually, I had saved that because I had wanted to build one of those myself. I was thinking of doing it at my parents' house since we always seem to end up over there, and my backyard is not big enough for this."

"That is very cool," I said as I studied it again. "If you were going to build this, how many swings would you build?"

"Seven. One for each of my siblings and their family, and one for my parents in the middle."

I sighed. I loved a man who thought of his family. "I love that idea. Would you help me design it for my backyard?" I hadn't meant to ask him, but the words slipped out. I lifted my face to him, and he was staring down at me as if he were surprised I had asked him.

I laughed and handed him back his phone. "I'm sorry. You are probably so busy. The last thing you have time for is to work on a project like that for someone you don't know."

"No, I'd like to." He seemed confused for a second and even shook his head as if to dislodge a thought, but then he grinned. "I'd like to."

"That would be awesome, but of course, I need to get a few other things done first inside the house," I told him as I shifted back around to the porch.

We discussed the back porch and my ideas for the garden and garage for the next few minutes. When we finished, we slipped back into the house and found Kayley on the phone in the kitchen. Maybe she did have to make a phone call and hadn't been giving us time to talk alone. Once in a while, I could be wrong.

"Do you want to see what else I have planned for the house?" I asked him as we walked into the kitchen.

"Sure, if you want to share them with me."

Ha! The man probably didn't realize this, but I would probably share just about anything with him. I was crushing big-time on my bestie's brother. I hadn't done that since high school.

I walked Brad through the house, pointing out things that I wanted to change, talking about colors, lighting, textures, and materials. It didn't take him long to start offering suggestions and ideas too, and I would seriously consider every one he made.

As we headed to my bedroom, he asked, "What brought you to Pennsylvania?"

"I hated the school I worked at and couldn't coach anymore, and since my ex-husband moved away, I didn't have any reason to hang in the area."

"You're divorced?"

"Yep, with two kids, what about you?" I knew that his wife was deceased, but I played it off like I didn't.

"I have two kids too. My wife passed a few years ago."

"Sorry to hear that. How old are your kids?"

He blinked at me and seemed confused for a moment before he grinned. "Tonya is twelve, and Tyler is ten."

I put my hand up. "Tonya Young is your daughter?"

"Um, I might be afraid to answer that." He snickered.

"I have her in my math class."

"You're Ms. Nickels?"

"Yes."

"Tonya thinks you're great. I didn't realize you were a teacher."

"Riley is the one that helped me get the job. She told me that they were looking for a math teacher at the middle school."

"You know Riley?"

"Honestly, I have met all your siblings and your parents. You were the last one for me to meet. I guess they saved the best for last."

He frowned. "The best for last?"

"Yeah, it's obvious that you and I have a lot in common, and I feel like I have known you forever, and we just met."

"Um…" He seemed uncomfortable, and I fought not to frown. What had I said to upset him?

I touched his arm. "I'm sorry, Brad. I didn't mean to make you uncomfortable. I was merely making a joke about it, but I do feel like the two of us could be good friends."

"Friends?"

"Yes, friends." I laughed. "I'm sorry if you thought I was hitting on you. The last thing I am looking for is a relationship with anyone." I sighed. "Although having sex again might be nice, but alas, a girl can dream."

He shifted, and I watched his Adam's apple bob as he scanned the inside of my room. "Friends would be nice."

"Good. I'm glad to hear that," I told him and headed toward my bathroom. I paused and looked back at him, smiling seductively. "Although, if you're ever interested in having sex, I wouldn't say no."

# CHAPTER SIX

## BRADLEY

*S*he did not just say that. I wanted to stuff my finger in my ear and wiggle it around to make sure I heard correctly.

I followed her into the bathroom, her words on a loop in my head. 'If you're ever interested in having sex, I wouldn't say no.' Holy crap! What would she say if I took her up on that? What would she do if I walked straight over to her and took her precious face in my hands and kissed her? What would she feel like as I lifted her in my arms and she locked her legs around my waist?

I shifted away, trying like hell to remove the image of her earlier state of undress from my mind. I'd seen more of this woman tonight than I had in several women in the last year. Was I just responding to her because I had seen her half dressed, or was it because she was so open—and flirting with me?

I wasn't sure, and it was making me nervous as hell. Already I'd offered to help her with the swing and fireplace in the backyard. If I didn't get away from this woman, I'd start volunteering to do a whole lot more, like take her up on that offer of sex.

No.

I could not do that.

Okay, I could, but I wouldn't. Focus here, Brad. Get your head out of your pants and back into the game.

"One of the guys that I work with, Milton, he's your plumber's son."

"Oh, Mr. Townsend, the man who called me cute as a button." She giggled, and I found myself entranced by the sound.

"He didn't say that to your face, did he?"

"Yep, he sure did, but that's not the worst thing I have heard. I'm used to people making comments about my size. From the back, I look like a teenager. Hell, even from below the neck, I look like a teenager, but my face belies my thirty-seven years."

I blinked. "You're thirty-seven years old? You can't be."

"I am, and I have a twelve-year-old and a ten-year-old to prove it."

I laughed. "Your kids are the same age as mine. Is your older one in your class?"

She pursed her lips momentarily. "No, my girls are back in New York with their grandparents finishing out the school year."

"Wow, that has to be hard," I commented. I could not imagine my kids not being around me every day. Maybe sometimes I wished they weren't, but not really.

"It is hard, and hence this overwhelming project to keep me busy."

"When are they coming to live with you again?"

"This summer."

"You are aware that you will never have all of this done by then, right? Not unless you hire a few guys to do it for you, and even then, it will be tight."

"I know that. My goal is to get the house cleaned and functional, like working water and no unwanted houseguests, and then work on the other things. I'd also love to have the kitchen done, but there is a lot to do there. First thing first is that I'll have to reconfigure the kitchen and find out where I'll need the new plumbing and electrical."

"I have a computer program that you can use that will help you design it so you can see what it would look like." Did I seriously just offer myself up to this woman again?

"Really? I have seen those programs where they render it, and you can see precisely what it's going to look like. I know you are busy, Brad, but would you mind helping me with that?"

Yes, I would mind. "No, not at all. I'd love to help." Who the hell was talking through my mouth?

She turned away from me, pointing at the shower, sighing. "That entire thing needs to come out, and I think I am going to remove the old cast iron tub and make it a large walk-in shower."

"Tiled?"

"Yes."

"Milton does that. Mr. Townsend's son. I'm sure he would love to help you."

"Do you know anyone who does stonework?"

"Yep, I have a guy for that too. Chester."

She eyed me carefully. "What about an electrician?"

"Pete."

"Look at you! You are fulfilling all my needs, and we aren't even in bed together yet."

I'm pretty sure my jaw dropped as she giggled and slipped around me and out of the room.

I stared at the age-cloudy mirror, wondering if she really was hitting on me. I had to be imagining it. I had been out of the dating field for so long that I wasn't sure what any of this meant, but there was no way she was openly flirting with me —right?

I followed her out of the bathroom and bedroom into the

hallway. She was standing at the top of the stairs waiting for me as she gnawed on her bottom lip.

As I approached her, I took in her trim legs and hips. Her brown hair was pulled back in a ponytail, and I suddenly had the urge to tug on her ponytail and expose her throat so I could taste the soft skin on my tongue.

She spun quickly, making me stop in my tracks a foot away. "I'm sorry about what I said in there. You are probably not used to someone being so direct."

"No, I'm not."

"I hope I didn't upset you. It's been a long time since I found myself attracted to someone, and you make me a little nervous. When I'm nervous, I tend to blurt things out."

"I make you nervous?" I wasn't touching the fact that she said she was attracted to me—nope.

She nodded. "Would you do me a favor?"

Both my brows popped high. I was pretty sure that if she asked me to get on my knees and beg, I would. This woman had a stronghold over me, and I wasn't sure what to think of that.

"Can you stand down one step for a moment?"

"The step? You want me to stand on the step? Why?"

"Because you're tall. I want to see you eye to eye."

I shook my head but slipped past her and went down a step. See—anything she asked. I kept my back to her, shifting to look over my shoulder.

"Turn around, silly." She laughed.

I turned around, holding on to the railing so I wouldn't fall backward and break my neck.

She shifted so she was on the edge of her step, and even though I was down one, I was still taller than her, but this did put our eyes—and mouths—at a more approachable distance.

"Thank you. It's much easier talking to someone when I don't have to crane my neck back."

"Okay, that makes sense. Now, what did you want to talk about?"

"I wanted to say thank you."

"For what?"

"For coming by here today and giving me ideas and advice."

"You're welcome."

"Were you serious about helping me design my kitchen?"

No. Ha! Who was I kidding? I was ready to help her with her entire house. Kayley had been right. One bat of her beautiful brown eyes, and I was willing to do anything for her. Why?

She leaned forward, and I froze. There was no way she was going to kiss me. She came closer, almost touching our noses together as she stared into my eyes.

"What are you doing?"

"Checking out your eye color."

"Why?"

"Because I happen to love brown, and your eyes are a pretty color."

I laughed. "They are brown."

"I said I liked brown."

"You did."

"I like your eyes, Bradley."

"I like your eyes, Nolan." I frowned slightly, and she leaned back and poked me in the nose with the tip of her finger.

"Seems weird to tell someone named Nolan that you like their eyes, doesn't it?"

"Kind of."

"You can call me Nola. Some of my friends do because they don't like Nolan."

"What do you want me to call you?"

She stared at me, another sexy smile slipping over her lips before she leaned forward, almost touching her mouth to mine. I was helpless to move as she stood there. A moment later, she shifted to the side toward my ear and whispered, "You can call me anything, as long as you whisper it into my ear."

She giggled again and brushed past me down the stairs. I was not wrong; she was most definitely flirting with me. I might have been out of the game for a while, but I wasn't an idiot.

Before I could get down the stairs, she disappeared into the kitchen, and I made my way slowly as I digested what she'd said. If she hadn't run away, I might have leaned forward and said something softly to her. Why, I didn't know, but it seemed like the right thing to do.

When I entered the kitchen, Cameron was in there with Kayley. "Hey, Brad, you getting the official tour?"

Nolan laughed. "He was getting the tour of this needs to happen and that needs to happen."

"It's a great house," I commented. "Once you get it done, it will be something."

"Yes, it will be."

"When did you want me to help you with the kitchen design?" I refrained from looking toward my sister because I knew she'd have a smug smile on her lips.

"Um, would you be available tomorrow late afternoon? We have soccer games in the morning, and I have a few errands to run after that."

"Yeah, I can do that. I'll just make sure my kids are taken care of."

"I'm sure Becky would be happy to keep them busy," Kayley offered.

"Let me see what they have planned. Can I give you a call later and confirm?"

"Is that your way of asking for my phone number?"

I laughed. "No, but having it would be a good idea."

"Alright," she commented and walked to the counter to write it down. She could have given it to me directly to put it in my phone, but whatever.

She folded the piece of paper and handed it to me, smiling sweetly. "Here you go. I'll see you tomorrow. Thanks for all your help, Brad."

"You're welcome." For two seconds, we stared at one another, and something I didn't understand passed between us.

"Thanks, Brad," Kayley said, and when I looked at her, I knew what she was thinking.

"See you later, Kay, Cam." I turned on my heel and hightailed it out of there. I wasn't in my truck when I got a message from my sister.

*I was right! One bat of those lashes, and you're a goner!*

I didn't bother to reply to her. I kind of hated that she was right. So, I had a soft spot for women who were petite and full of positive energy. It didn't hurt that she loved to work with her hands and had so many of the same ideas that I would have had for the place.

As I pulled away, I almost wished that I had thought of looking into buying the property. It really would have made an excellent investment and been something I could slowly work on over the years. Plus, the property itself was incredible.

I thought again of the swings and fireplace design that I had shown her. My current backyard wasn't big enough for that, and my parents' backyard wasn't set up for something that shape or size, but Nolan's yard would have been perfect.

Well, I hoped that she decided to do something like that, maybe on a smaller scale. I would be happy to help her build it so that I could see it done. Perhaps I'd even get a chance to sit on one of the swings and enjoy a fire with her.

I shook my head at myself. She might have been flirting with me, but that didn't mean anything. For all I knew, she might flirt with everyone. That could just be the kind of person she was. Or perhaps she was flirting with me to get my help on her home. I nodded to myself as I stopped at the stop sign.

That's what she was doing. Kayley probably told her that if

she flirted with me, I'd help her out. It kind of made me not want to help, but remembering the way she had stared at me on the stairs and whispered in my ear, made me wonder.

It wasn't until I was home that I unfolded the piece of paper she had given me. It not only included her number but a short note.

*Brad, thanks for helping. I look forward to getting to know you better. The offer still stands. Nolan*

I read it three times, wondering if she meant that or if she just wanted to entice me for the free help. I guess only time would tell.

# CHAPTER SEVEN

NOLAN

*C*am left shortly after Brad, and Kayley and I got back to cleaning. We were working on the master bedroom floor. The two of us were down on our hands and knees, scrubbing and scraping at the residue left over from years of foot traffic and neglect. Already it was looking better, and I knew that once I had it stained and polished, it would be amazing.

"You and Brad hit it off pretty well," Kayley commented as she used a sand block wedge on the floor.

"I guess we did." I looked at her. "You could have warned me that he was as good-looking as he was."

Kayley snorted. "He is my brother. I don't think of him that way."

"How could you not? I mean, all of your brothers are attractive men, but Brad is downright gorgeous."

Kayley lifted her head to me. "You really think so?"

"Um, yes! When I walked in and saw him in my kitchen, I was tempted to keep taking my clothes off and attack him right then and there. I can't remember the last time I had such a visceral reaction to a man."

"Yeah, well, be careful, or you might scare him away. He's

pretty old-fashioned, and I know he hasn't dated much since Cheryl died."

"You said she had cancer?"

"Yeah, when they found it, it was stage four already. Not much that the doctors could do."

"That sucks. I'm sure it's been hard on him."

"It has been, but it's been like six years since she passed. Brad needs to move on."

"You can't rush that kind of thing, Kayley. I'm sure when he is ready, he will." I gnawed on my bottom lip. "I kind of propositioned him. Is that bad?"

Her head snapped up, and she leaned back on her knees. "You what?"

"I told him if he was interested in having sex, I wouldn't be against it."

Kayley cackled out a laugh. "Oh, my god! Brad was probably ready to run screaming for the hills."

"I don't think so. He had the opportunity to walk away after I said it, but he didn't. He did seem a bit uncomfortable, but he didn't tell me no."

"He has better manners." She paused. "God, I hate to say this about my brother, but if you can get him in bed, go for it. The man hasn't been with a woman in forever."

"How do you know he hasn't been with someone else?"

"Wes told me. Brad and Wes are close."

I pondered something for a moment and then asked, "Would you be upset if I slept with your brother?"

She shook her head. "No. I think it would be good for him, and I told him that I thought you two would be good together."

"Wait! I'm not talking about having a relationship. I was merely thinking of a good time in bed. It's been a while for me too, not six years, but long enough."

She shrugged. "Who knows. You two might enjoy having sex together so much that it becomes a relationship. That is kind of what happened with Cam and me. Originally, I was only interested in the pleasure of a younger man, but then he proved to be much more than I anticipated."

"Yeah, well, I'm not looking for a husband. I just want someone to share some steamy nights with or someone who can help unwind the stress."

"Whatever works for you, but Nolan, be careful with Brad. I'm afraid that if you two do sleep together, he might see it as more than it is. Make sure he knows exactly how you feel and that it's a casual thing and not the start of a relationship."

"Okay, I can do that," I told her.

After that, we moved the conversation on to other things, and it wasn't until later that night when I was lying in the guest room at Kayley's that I thought back over the conversation. I guess Kayley was right about being open and honest with him from the start. It would be the most intelligent way to handle things. I honestly didn't want a relationship, but sex, oh, hell yeah! I was all about some sexy time in the bedroom.

On Saturday, the soccer teams had two games. I was the head coach on the girls' team and assistant coach on the boys'. Even though I was assistant coach to them, I found that I did most of the coaching, as the head coach was preoccupied with his cellphone almost the entire game. Good job, Coach.

I didn't mind, though. After the games, one we lost and one we won, I hit a few stores for things that I needed for my projects this week and then stopped by the grocery store for dinner. I didn't dare use the stove. The appliance was so ancient that I'd be afraid to turn it on, but I was able to pick up a rotisserie chicken that could be eaten cold along with some side salads and fruit to pick at for dessert.

I had planned to run back to Kayley's house to shower but

found I was out of time. Brad had called me yesterday, and after a short conversation, we'd decided on four o'clock. I figured it would take us an hour to two hours to complete the kitchen remodel design, and then we could eat. Truth be told, I was more excited about seeing him than I was about redesigning my kitchen. It should have been the other way around, but I couldn't help myself.

For the last few days, I'd had quite a few little fantasies about Brad and I having sex in different parts of my house. I was jumping the gun here. I might have this conversation with him, and it might totally turn him off.

I could only hope that it did the opposite.

I had just carried everything inside when I heard a truck in the driveway. Little butterflies took flight in my belly, and I found myself grinning like a schoolgirl at the prospect of an exciting evening.

I met him on the porch and let my eyes drift over his form-fitting t-shirt and denim-clad legs. The temptation to lick my lips was strong, but I behaved myself.

"Hey! Thanks for coming over. You have no idea how much I appreciate your help, Brad."

He smiled, and the lines beside his eyes were more pronounced. Why were those lines so sexy to me? "My pleasure, Nolan."

Oh, I'd like it to be *my* pleasure that made him smile, but I held that bit of information back.

"How was your day?" I asked him as he reached the porch.

"It's been busy. I heard the girls won today."

"They did." I cocked my head. "How did you hear that?"

"Tonya was there watching a friend play."

"Oh, I didn't see her. I was focused on the kids. Why doesn't she play?"

"She wanted to, but she was afraid that she wouldn't be good enough."

"That's a shame. You only get better when you practice. Maybe I can talk to Tonya and get her to change her mind."

He laughed as he took the steps up. "Yeah, good luck with that. She's pretty hardheaded."

"Who does she get that from, you or her mother?"

He smirked. "Maybe a little from both of us."

I chuckled for a moment. "Well, come on in. Let's get this party started. I'm excited to see what we can accomplish."

"I think once you put it on paper, it's going to be great. I was thinking a lot about you—um, your initial design ideas, and I think your concept is going to work well."

I stopped and spun on him, grinning victoriously at him. "Oh, so you admit to thinking about me, huh?"

"Your kitchen design—I was thinking about your kitchen design."

For a few seconds, we studied one another, and I saw the lie in his eyes. Maybe he didn't want to think about me in a personal way, but he had been. The little schoolgirl in me wanted to giggle and bounce on my toes, but I didn't.

"Yeah, okay," I replied saucily and led him into the kitchen. He set his laptop on the counter and turned it on. While it was booting up, he surveyed the room.

"Where do you want to start?"

Would it be too forward to say with him naked? Probably. "Well, how about we figure out the measurements of the new area first. If we took that wall down, I could shift that counter out to open this area. I think it will give me enough room to allow me to add an island, plus have additional storage underneath."

"Alright. We can do that. How about I call out measurements, and you write them down?"

"Perfect." I collected my notepad and a pen and stood back as he walked around taking the measurements. I found myself rather intrigued by how his biceps and back muscles under his shirt moved and I kept shifting on my feet to keep from attacking him. Was it too early to have that conversation about sex?

I felt like a horny college student as I eyed the man in front of me, wishing he'd give me some kind of sign that he was interested. So far, he had been polite and professional, and I didn't want either of those. I wanted dirty and sexy.

Once we had all the measurements, we talked about the counters and island and where the appliances could go. I forced myself to focus on the kitchen and not the bedroom—or at least not him naked.

With all that decided, he returned to his computer and started working.

"Is your son as hardheaded as your daughter?"

He lifted his gaze to mine momentarily, as if confused by the change in conversation before giving me a half grin. "No, he's pretty easygoing."

"My girls are more like their father than me. They aren't as outgoing, at least not yet. I hope that changes. I think kids nowadays need to be outgoing if they want to get anywhere in life."

"What makes you say that?" he asked as he worked on his laptop.

Although he wasn't looking at me, I shrugged and then turned and popped my butt up on the counter beside him. I saw him shift his gaze toward my legs and then away quickly.

"Things are different than they were when we grew up. Now life demands that they take charge of things, and I think too many kids just kind of ride the winds without making any firm decisions. They do what they have to because they have to, not because they want to, or because they are driven to do it."

He finally lifted his gaze to mine. "What kinds of things are you talking about?"

"Relationships, colleges, even sports. They do things because they are told to do them. Parents push kids to do sports because they want them to do them, not because the kids want to. You'd be surprised how many kids I have coached that didn't want to be on the field, and almost as many kids that I know want to play, but their parents say no. Sadly, they don't push back—or it falls on deaf ears at home. Then the kids pick college majors because their parents expect them to do as they are told, not because it's what they want to do. It's almost like the parents are projecting their own missed hopes on their kids and expect them to do everything that they should have done growing up."

He chuckled slightly. "I wouldn't do that to my kids."

"No, you might not, but many other parents do. I think your family is a bit different than the traditional family out there."

He cocked his head as he studied me. "What makes you say that?"

"Your parents are still married. That right there is a feat. None of your siblings are divorced. The only reason you are single is that your wife died. Otherwise, you'd still be happily married."

"You don't know that."

"You don't think you would still be happily married to Cheryl if she hadn't died?"

He pursed his lips and returned his focus to the computer. "I don't know. I'd like to think we might have—"

"Might have what?"

"Nothing, never mind."

"No, don't backtrack on that. You were going to say something. Tell me, Brad."

"It's not important."

I laughed. "If you are trying so hard not to say it, it must have been important—at least to you."

He stared at his screen for a few moments. "Things weren't always great with my wife."

"Is any marriage one hundred percent happy?"

He lifted his gaze to mine. "No, but a couple of days before she found out that she had cancer, I told her I wanted a divorce."

That raised my brows slightly. "What did she think of that?"

"She agreed. Then two days later, she found out she had cancer, and neither of us spoke of the divorce again." He was quiet for a moment. "None of my family knows about that, so please do not say anything."

"I won't. May I ask why your marriage was going down the tubes?"

He took a long deep breath and released it. "Because she said she wasn't in love with me anymore, and she had met someone else."

Ouch! "What did you think of that?"

"I think, I don't want to talk about this anymore." His voice was low as he typed a few things on the keyboard.

"Okay, do you want to talk about when we are going to have sex?"

He practically choked on his tongue. "How about we talk about your kitchen?"

I leaned closer to him. "I don't think that will be as much fun, but whatever you want, Brad."

# CHAPTER EIGHT

## BRADLEY

*CW*hat I wanted was to step in between her legs and kiss her. I wasn't going to do that, though. Ever since I had left her the other day, I had been thinking about her nonstop. I hadn't thought about a woman like that since I'd met Cheryl, and I wasn't sure I wanted to have thoughts like that ever again.

"The kitchen would be a safer conversation."

She grinned at me, and I loved the way her eyes lit up. "You like to play things safe, don't you?"

"Most of the time."

"Do you ever *not* play it safe?"

Did I? Not really. "It's been a long time."

"Don't you think you owe it to yourself to get a little out of control once in a while?"

I laughed. "Not when I have two young kids."

"Who aren't here right now. I get it, Brad. I'm usually a lot more adult when my kids are around, but they aren't, and I can let my hair down a little because of that."

I shifted on my feet, fighting the urge to step over to her and taste her lips as we stared at one another.

"I'm not asking for a relationship. In fact, I'm not interested in one, but would it be so wrong for two consenting adults to have an intimate relationship to satisfy a physical need?"

Holy crap! Where did this woman come from? I swallowed. "No, but I'm not one for one-night stands."

"It's the afternoon. It wouldn't be a one-night stand." I tucked my chin down to my chest and stared at her as she laughed. "So we can have sex multiple times on multiple days, and then it really wouldn't be a one-night stand. It would be an affair of sorts."

"You really are always this direct with your thoughts."

"Yep. I don't like to mince words. Life is too short, as you already know."

"I can't. I'm sorry, Nolan." I stared at the computer for a moment. "If that is why you wanted my help, then I'm sorry. I can't help you." I started to close my computer, and she grabbed my wrist.

"Don't."

I stared at her hand, feeling the warmth of her fingers travel up my arm.

"Stay. If you only want to help me with my design, then I want your help. I'm not going to apologize for finding you attractive. Honestly, I was hoping that it was mutual, but obviously, it's not. So, I'll just shut up and behave myself. I promise."

Did I want her to behave herself? Part of me wanted her to keep egging me on until I got the nerve to kiss her, but another part of me said, walk away now because this woman will be trouble to my heart and soul.

She squeezed my forearm once and then slowly let it go. I watched her hand drift back to her leg and then stared at her thigh. She was wearing shorts, and she had toned thighs that made my hands itch to touch.

I began to lift my gaze, taking in the t-shirt that she wore and the swell of her small breasts under it. I swallowed again as

I got to her neck and fought not to dive toward it. As my gaze reached her face, she stared at me, her lips parted, her bright-brown eyes wide.

Before I could think, I sidestepped, and she shifted her legs wider to allow me to fit between them fully. She remained still, waiting patiently for me to do something. For two seconds, we stared at one another, and then I curled my hand around her neck, pulling her forward.

Her arms wrapped around my shoulders as our lips met, and she opened immediately, swirling her tongue against mine. She shifted her body, pressing her chest against mine as the kiss deepened, and I felt myself falling into her.

I hadn't kissed a woman in many years. It unleashed a passion and need that I hadn't felt in way too long. She whimpered slightly as she squeezed me tighter to her body, and my hands roamed over her back, aching to touch more.

I slipped my mouth off hers, moving it down to her neck as she leaned back, a sigh leaving her lips as I tasted her salty skin. One of her hands clenched a fistful of my hair, holding me against her throat as I nibbled softly.

Her legs locked around my waist, and I pressed my hips against her as fire fueled my blood.

"Whoops!" A voice behind us startled us both, and I jerked back, instantly reaching around to unlock Nolan's ankles. "Sorry, I didn't mean to interrupt," Kayley said.

I glanced at my sister, who was grinning from ear to ear as I shifted away. I stood in front of my computer to hide my now tight jeans. Holy crap, what had I been thinking?

I hadn't been thinking. For once, I had been feeling, and all that I had felt just made me want to feel more. Damn, Kayley, for her interruption, but at the same time, I was glad that she had. The last thing I needed to do was have crazy unprotected sex with this woman on her warped kitchen counter. God, when was the last time I carried a condom with me? It must have been fifteen years since I'd tucked one of those little squares in my wallet.

"What are you doing here?" Nolan asked her as she hopped off the counter and approached my sister. Was that a bit of tension in her words for being interrupted?

"You left the counter and cabinet swatches at home. I thought you might need it while you two are working on your kitchen."

"Oh, crap! You're right. We need them. We aren't to that part yet, so I hadn't realized. Thank you."

"I'll leave you to your work," Kayley said. "Have fun, Brad!"

"Bye, Kay," I remarked over my shoulder, not looking at her. I didn't need to see the I-told-you-so look in her eye.

I heard the two of them speaking quietly by the front door, and then the door clicked closed.

Nolan returned and put her hand on my back. "So—where were we?"

I laughed slightly. "We were going to discuss the placement of your appliances."

She hopped back onto the counter. "I don't think that is the placement we were working on."

I pursed my lips, inhaled through my nose, and then looked at her after I released it. "But we should be talking about the placement of your appliances."

She tilted her head to the side. "Does it bother you that your sister saw you kissing me?"

"No," I said, but I averted my eyes because it did bother me.

"Yes, it did. Why? Why would kissing another single woman be a problem?"

"Because you are her friend, Nolan."

"So, she told me she didn't have any problems with me sleeping with you."

I jerked back slightly. "You talked to my sister about us having sex? Don't you think that was a little premature?"

She shook her head. "No. I asked her because I didn't want to step over any lines in our friendship. If she had said she wasn't comfortable with it, I wouldn't have brought it up to you again."

"Again?"

"I told you yesterday that I'd be willing to sleep with you."

"Nolan, I'm sorry." I closed the computer and retreated as I picked it up. "I don't think I can help you. You're a smart woman, so I'm sure you can figure it out on your own."

"You're going to leave because I talked to your sister about having sex with you?"

"No, I'm going to leave because sex between us is not going to happen. I was wrong to kiss you, wrong to come here when I knew this might happen."

She hopped off the counter and glared up at me. "Then why did you?"

"Because part of me thought I might be making it all up, and there was no way you'd be interested in someone like me."

"I'm interested in having sex with someone like you," she retorted.

"Yeah, but I don't just have sex, Nolan."

She crossed her arms over her chest. "Fine." I watched her for a moment as several emotions flitted over her face. Finally, she sighed. "I owe you an apology."

"No, you don't."

"I do. I was very forward, but I told you before that it's been a while since I was attracted to someone. I thought maybe that was reciprocated."

"It is," I told her without thinking, then added, "But that doesn't mean that I can just have sex with you because I'm in the mood. I wasn't brought up like that. I have relations with people that I care about."

She nodded. "Alright, I will accept that, but will you please stay and help me? I could use your assistance, and I promise that I will behave myself."

I wasn't sure she was capable of that, but I wanted to stay.

"I promise I will not make any more innuendos or tempt you anymore."

Well, that was a lie. The woman was a walking temptation. "Alright, as long as you promise."

She gave me a sly smile. "Although, you have to admit, that kiss was pretty damn good."

I laughed as I shook my head. "Yeah, I guess it was."

"Just guess? Come on, that kiss had to have made your top ten at least."

"Well, considering the fact that I have probably only kissed seven or eight females in my life that way, that would be true."

Her eyes popped out of her head. "Are you serious?"

"Yes. I told you. I wasn't brought up to sleep around. I only kissed women I was involved with."

"Wow, okay. Then I'm happy to tell you that I have kissed more than ten men before, and you are still in my top ten."

I chuckled. "I guess that is nice to hear."

"So, get your computer back up, and let's put some appliances into my kitchen, shall we?"

"That we can do." I set the computer back on the countertop, and within a few moments, she was all business. As we discussed counters and locations, she walked around and pointed things out while I worked on the computer. We figured out the area of everything, along with where new pipes would need to go and electrical wiring would have to be run.

Ninety minutes later, we had a rendering of her kitchen and she stood beside me grinning at the screen. "I love it!"

"It looks pretty awesome. Not much that I would have done differently."

She stared up at me. "What would you have done differently?"

"Probably different cabinets and counters." I pointed to the booklets she had lying on the counter that Kayley had dropped off. "I'd go for something a bit more rustic, but I like what you chose."

"You think more rustic would be better?"

"That's my taste, not yours. This house has a very rustic feel to it, especially with some of the things you have said you were going to do with it."

She pondered that, moving her mouth back and forth, and I was suddenly tempted to capture those lips again, but I held myself back. Over the last hour and a half, I had enjoyed working with her. She had an eye for design and a flair in her personality that beckoned to me.

I wasn't sure if it was because she'd admitted that she was attracted to me or because I was attracted to her. For the first time in a long time, I wanted to throw caution to the wind and just let myself enjoy. If only I'd had a condom with me, I might have.

Nah, I probably would have chickened out, but it was a nice fantasy to have.

After we finished, she brought out the food, and we went to sit on the back porch and eat. The sun was setting, and the temperatures were cooling down slightly, but it was still a pleasant spring evening.

Between the food and the company, I was finding myself oddly relaxed as I scanned her backyard. "Did you give any more thought to the swings and firepit?"

"I did," she said excitedly, turning to me. "Do you still want to help me with that?"

"Sure," I replied without a thought. I locked eyes with her, knowing that if this woman asked me again to have sex with her, I probably would have said to hell with the condom and attacked her right there on her back porch.

# CHAPTER NINE

## NOLAN

*I*t hadn't been fair of me to throw myself at him. Not before I knew him more. After our talk, I did everything I could to make him comfortable and forced myself to put my hormones on the back burner. It was difficult, but not impossible.

While we went through ideas for my kitchen, I got a look into the way Brad's mind worked, and I had to admit that I liked it—and appreciated it. I was glad that he had given me another chance, and I did feel slightly sinister for the way I had acted earlier.

Brad's comment about how he would have added cabinets and counters that were more rustic had me contemplating my original choices. I did want the house to have a rustic, homey feel to it, and his choices would reflect that better than mine, but I sure did love the ones I had picked out. I'd have to sleep on it and see what I thought tomorrow.

"What are your kids doing tonight?"

"They are with Wes and Charlotte. I forgot that the circus was in town, and Charlotte wanted to take them along with her daughter, Marisol, to see it. They wanted to treat Marisol to something special since she's been so good with her baby brother, Michael."

"How old is Marisol?"

"I think she's seven, might be eight. I have a hard time remembering how old my kids are." He laughed softly, and I stared at his profile.

"What time will they be home tonight?"

He shifted as if he were slightly uncomfortable. "Um, they are staying overnight with them."

Aw, man! The temptation to say something like, then we have all night to get our groove on was trying to spring from my mouth, but I painfully held it back.

"Do you have someplace else to be tonight?" I asked.

He turned to me, his reply soft. "No, and you promised—"

I grabbed his arm as I laughed. "I know what I promised, Brad. I'm not going to entice you into my wicked web. As tempting as that might be. Do you want to know what I was going to suggest?"

"Maybe?"

"Any chance you have a sledgehammer in your truck?"

He nodded as confusion crossed his features. "Of course."

"Want to do some demolition on my kitchen? We could knock down that wall, get those old cabinets out of there. It would be a great way to work off this sexual tension crackling between us."

He chuckled. "You want to tear that down tonight?"

I shrugged, noting that he ignored my comment about the sexual tension. "Sure, why not! Plus, with you here, I'd feel better if something happened."

"What do you mean if something happened?"

"Like the ceiling started to fall in on us."

He laughed loudly. "You want me to get killed along with you, is that it?"

"No, I just mean that if things start to go sideways, I'm sure you will have a better idea of what to do."

He watched me for a moment, and I remained still as he did. I knew he was thinking of more than just tearing down a wall, and I hoped he was considering kissing me again—or more.

"You really want to take down a wall tonight?"

"Yes!" I replied excitedly. "I've never done that kind of demolition before. I've removed and replaced toilets and vanities but never removed a wall."

He shook his head. "You do remind me a lot of Kay."

"That's what bonded us. We met in a home repair store. I asked her opinion on something, and we got to talking. One thing led to another, and we became great friends."

"I'm glad you are."

"Me, too. So, what do you say? Want to play demolition man?"

"Sure, let's do it."

"You grab the sledgehammer, and I'll put this food away."

As he walked away, I watched his backside until he stepped around the corner. Why was I so attracted to this man? He was the complete opposite of any other man I'd been interested in. Most of them had been businessmen.

I packed up the uneaten food, put it back into the cooler, and then returned to the kitchen. Before Brad joined me, I dug around in the dining room where I was storing all my tools and found my work gloves and a hammer, along with protective goggles.

I heard him behind me and turned to look back as he eyed me from head to toe. "Good, you have goggles. I brought a pair in case you didn't. Do you have a dust mask?"

"Um, no. I forgot to pick those up."

He handed me one. "You should wear a dust mask with everything you do in here, especially tearing out or scraping. You have no idea what it is you are stirring up."

"I'll make sure to pick some up," I told him as I adjusted it over my face. He was also wearing gloves, goggles, and a mask, and he held the sledgehammer out to me.

"The first crack is yours."

I was grinning like an idiot behind my mask as I took the heavy tool from his hands. "What should I go for first?"

"You are going to want to start with the counter, strike it from underneath, so it pops off the counter bases."

I tried to do it, and even though I was strong for my size, I couldn't get the leverage to make the countertop pop. I handed the sledge back to Brad. "You do this part. I'll tear down the wall."

It took him two strikes to get it to pop, and then he was on the other side, working it off there. A few minutes later, the two of us hoisted the warped counter off the bases and down the hall to the front door.

The more we removed from the room, the more I grinned behind my mask. I loved that I could take part in this and be remodeling this kitchen on my own. Well, with a bit of help from professionals, but mostly on my own.

Brad and I worked for almost two hours on tearing all the cabinets and counters out. We even moved the old stove, sink, fridge, and dishwasher into the front hallway to be disposed of later. As we worked, we shared stories about our kids—mostly his. What they liked, what they didn't. Favorite subjects in school, plans for the future, and so on. It was an easy conversation, and it made the two hours fly by.

I removed my mask as I stood back and scanned the room. "Wow, it looks better already."

"It does," he replied.

I collected two water bottles, and we took a break, both of us looking at our cellphones. I laughed when I saw the message from Kayley. *You guys come up for air yet?*

I turned around and took a picture of the empty kitchen,

then sent her a message. *We haven't stopped since you left.* After a moment, I sent the picture.

*Holy smokes! Did you do that alone, or is Brad there with you?*

*We designed the kitchen, ate dinner, and then he stayed to help me do some demo.*

*Wow! I'm super impressed. You guys almost done for the night?*

*Don't wait up,* I replied.

She sent me back laughing emojis, and I put my phone back in the other room as Brad typed something on his.

"What do we do about the electrical in the wall?"

"Well, the safest thing is to cap it off and then cut the board around the outlets to see what direction the wires are going. We don't want to strike the wall with the sledgehammer and end up yanking the electrical wires down from upstairs or electrocuting ourselves."

"Yeah, I might like pain, but shock therapy is out of the question." He agreed, and I went to get a screwdriver.

"Do you have wire nuts?"

"Um, I don't know. Let me look in this box. If I have any, they will be in here."

"Are all of these tools yours?"

I glanced back over my shoulder to see him leaning against the threshold of the room, his arms crossed over his chest. "Yeah. I have accumulated them over the years. It's funny"—I moved to dig around inside the box—"when I got divorced, I made sure that I got all the tools in the settlement. My ex, Rick, started fighting me for them until I reminded him that I was the one that fixed everything in the house—not him."

He chuckled, and as I peered back at him, I noticed him checking me out from the back. There was hope yet. I finally located the wire nuts. "Got them!"

"Anything you don't have in here?"

"Oh, there is a lot that I don't have, but I learned early on as I did jobs around my house to repair things, to buy the correct tools for each job."

"Smart idea."

"I have those sometimes," I told him sassily as I passed by his side into the kitchen.

He watched over my shoulder as I did the work, giving me suggestions as I did it, and once the wires were capped, we cut a section off on the board to see where the wires went. Once we knew the path, we stood at the other end, and he handed me back the sledge.

"I'm pretty sure you can do some damage to this wall all by yourself."

"Let's see." I picked up the sledgehammer and stood back, taking a deep breath as I pulled it back and then let it loose. It went right through the drywall into the kitchen, and I whooped and laughed. When I turned, I found Brad grinning at me, his cellphone out as he held it up.

"Did you take a picture of that?"

He grinned. "Better. I took a video. Keep going."

I did. After a few minutes, I set the sledgehammer down and started tearing the wallboard away with my hands. Brad jumped in to help me, and before long, we were down to the studs. He studied them for a few minutes and made sure that they weren't holding anything up, and then we began to work on them. Instead of smashing those out, we dismantled them piece by piece.

It was close to midnight when I stood in my kitchen, happy as a clam. Brad came to stand beside me, and I glanced his way. His t-shirt was filthy, and I looked down at myself. "Wow, I'm a mess."

"Please don't go whipping your shirt off right now," he commented huskily, and I peered his way to find his eyes closed as if he were praying.

I laughed. "I'm not going to take my shirt off, Brad. You're safe to open your eyes." I stepped away, slightly confused. "You know, most men would be like, 'take it off, let me check you out,' but not you."

I expected him to say something, but he didn't. I shifted to look at him, and he was watching me.

"What?"

"I'd like nothing more than to check you out, Nolan, but I'm afraid if I do, looking won't be enough."

My breath caught in my lungs, and took a second to start moving again. "You know I wouldn't mind that."

His gaze slipped down my body and back up, a lazy smile caressing his lips. "I wouldn't either, but I think we both could use a shower before we even think to go there."

"Well, I'd invite you into mine, but it doesn't work."

"That's probably a good thing."

"Or not," I said, and then I yawned.

"We should probably call it a night."

"Yeah, I guess so." I glanced around, suddenly feeling exhausted. "Let me check upstairs to make sure all the lights are off, and then I'll walk you out."

He laughed. "How about you check for the lights, and then I walk *you* out to your car?"

"Deal." I hustled up the stairs, making sure lights were off, and windows were closed, and then I was back down a minute later. Brad had collected his tools and was waiting by the front door, the lights in the kitchen off.

"What time are you coming back tomorrow?"

"I will probably be here by seven, maybe eight at the latest since it's so late tonight. I have a lot to do tomorrow, and Mr. Townsend asked if he could come back and check a few more things before he starts on Monday. I need to find an electrician to come in this week and look at the electricity. Once the pipes are replaced, and the wiring is redone, I can move in."

"You need any help tomorrow? The kids won't be home until around one."

"Are you serious? You are willing to help me more?"

"I don't have any other plans in the morning. What were you going to work on? I could repair the ceiling where we removed the wall."

"You know what, Brad? I think you are my new best friend! I'd love for you to come by in the morning."

We stepped down the stairs and walked toward the driveway. "Then I'll see you in the morning." He glanced at his watch. "How about seven-thirty?"

"Perfect," I told him.

We stared at one another for a long moment, and before I could overthink it, I popped up on my toes and placed a quick kiss on his lips. "Night, Brad."

"Good night, Nolan."

I watched him walk to his truck, and as he got in, I saw the grin on his face in the light of the dome. It was very similar to the one I wore on my face.

# CHAPTER TEN

## BRADLEY

*I* was afraid to admit it, but I liked Nolan. I loved her energy and her will to do just about anything. I always did have a thing for women who wanted to get dirty. Cheryl had been the opposite. She preferred to stay perfectly manicured and let me do all the dirty work. It was no wonder our marriage went to hell.

As I showered at home and climbed into bed, I pondered over the differences between the two women. Cheryl had been more like my sister Riley. She liked clothes and makeup. She preferred to go out and have fun with friends. Before we'd had kids, I would join her sometimes, but after they were born, I found myself more and more at home with them while she painted the town red.

I didn't mind. I wasn't into dancing and drinking until I couldn't stand up straight. I preferred to stay with the kids, read them a story, or play a game. Then I read a book myself or watched a home improvement show to get design ideas.

It wasn't that Cheryl was a bad mother. She was great with the kids when she was home. She just wanted more out of her life than to be a wife and mother, and that's how she ended up meeting someone else.

I'd had a feeling for a while that she'd been seeing someone, but I didn't want to admit it. She spent a lot of time texting someone and was quiet when I was around. She'd come home later and head right into the shower while I pretended to be asleep. When our sex life completely dried up, I was all but sure.

When I finally confronted her, she hadn't denied it. She'd taken a deep breath and said that she had met someone else and that she cared for him. I had asked her if she wanted a divorce, and she'd lifted her chin and said yes.

Part of me had been crestfallen, but another part of me was glad that our marriage was going to be over, and most of the blame would fall on her. I didn't look forward to admitting failure to my family, but at least I would have a chance in the future to find someone else to love and maybe have the family life that I had always dreamed of having.

The kind of family life that my siblings were all now enjoying.

At seven-thirty, I showed back up at Nolan's place. I knocked but could hear music playing inside, so I let myself in and found her in the kitchen, singing and wiggling her hips as she swept up the mess from last night.

"Morning."

She jumped and spun. "I didn't hear you come in. Good morning." She pulled the mask off her face and grinned at me. "How are you today?"

"I'm good. Did you get any sleep? You look like you have done a lot here already."

"I got here about an hour ago. I woke up around five-thirty and hopped right out of bed, excited by all that we did yesterday."

"Five-thirty? And you had the energy to hop out of bed?" I chuckled. "I dragged my ass out of bed at quarter to seven."

"When I crash, I crash. I was asleep before my head hit the pillow, and I didn't even move all night." She put her mask back in place and started sweeping again. "I'm one of those people that as soon as my eyes open, I am wide awake and ready to get moving. I can't lie in bed and lounge around."

Another difference her and Cheryl had with one another. "What would you like me to do?"

"Did you eat?"

"No."

"Want to run down to the coffee shop and grab breakfast and coffee? I only had one small cup; I could use another."

"Sure, I'll go down to Coral's. What would you like?"

"What's good there? I have had their coffee, but nothing else besides a cookie."

"Coral makes delicious breakfast sandwiches."

"Okay, I'll take one."

"Bagel, toast, English muffin, or croissant?"

"Oh, croissants, huh? I'll take one of those."

"What kind of meat? Sausage, bacon, Canadian bacon, scrapple, or Spam?"

She scrunched up her face so much I could tell even though she was wearing a mask. "Surprise me with anything other than scrapple—or Spam. Those are just gross."

"What do you have against those?"

"Scrapple is made from all the yucky parts that don't fit into anything else, and it smells horrible, and I'm just not a fan of Spam."

"You don't know what you're missing."

She eyed me sternly. "I'll take your word for it."

"Cheese?"

"Yes."

"Alright. What do you want in your coffee?"

"Black, and just pick up some sugar packets. If they have raw sugar, I'll take that."

"Anything else?"

"Yeah, pick me out a donut that has chocolate on it."

"Okay—"

"And do they have fruit cups?"

"Didn't we have leftover fruit from last night?"

"Oh, yeah, we did, but I forgot to take it to Kayley's, so it might be a little ripe from being in the cooler all night." She dug around in her pocket and pulled out money as she came to stand in front of me, holding out thirty dollars.

"Put your money away."

"No, you are helping me. The least I can do is pay for food."

"Who said I'm not going to charge you later?"

She pulled her mask down and tilted her chin up to see me better. "Are you going to charge me later, Brad?"

"Maybe not in currency," I replied softly.

"Yeah? In what? Sex?" Her brows rose, and she looked hopeful. Man, I wanted to kiss her and give in to her wishes.

"No, I was thinking more along the lines of letting me use those swings sometime and maybe a homecooked dinner."

She rolled her eyes and chuckled. "Fine, but I still want to pay for breakfast."

"Alright." I took the money she held out, and before I could think more on it, I leaned down and kissed her softly, once. She looked almost as surprised as I was that I had done that, but a moment later, she winked and stepped away.

I was grinning like an idiot as I went back to my truck. It had felt so natural to do that.

I was back thirty minutes later and found Kayley's car in the driveway. I was slightly disappointed that my sister was here, but I forced myself to keep a smile on my face as I went in and found not only Kay there but Cam too, inspecting our work from the previous night.

"Food!" Nolan called out as soon as I came in.

"Hey, guys." I tried not to be embarrassed as I looked at my sister, but the smile on her face made my cheeks warm a bit. "If I had known you were going to be here, I would have gotten you something."

"That's okay," Cameron replied. "We've already eaten."

"You guys got a lot done last night," my sister stated. "Do you have the drawing of what it's going to look like?"

"My computer is in my truck," I told her.

"Okay, after you eat, you can show me."

Cameron and Kayley had brought coffee travel mugs with them, and they joined us on the back porch as we sat on the steps and ate our breakfast.

"I haven't even slept here, and I've already had two picnics on the back porch," Nolan commented after she scarfed down her sandwich. "That was good."

"I should have gotten you a second one."

"Did you get my fruit?" she asked.

I nodded as I pulled it out of the bag. "And you still have your donut here."

She winked at me. "Saving that for break time."

As we finished our breakfast, we made a plan for the work to be done. Mr. Townsend would be here around eleven to go over the pipes again and make sure he had everything on his list that he needed. I pulled out my phone and sent a couple of text messages to Pete, Milton, Chester, and Chad to see if they could stop by and heard back from all of them within a few moments.

Kayley and Nolan were looking over my computer rendering, discussing the cabinets, and Cameron helped me with the ceiling. I used a sheet of drywall that Nolan had delivered for repairs, and Cam and I worked on patching the ceiling. From time to time, I'd glance at Nolan, and we'd share a look and sometimes a smile.

The more times we glanced at one another, the higher I felt that sexual tension climbing. At least Kayley didn't seem to have noticed, or if she did, she wasn't saying anything for now.

At eleven-fifteen, Mr. Townsend showed up, and Milton was with him. Kayley and Cam started going around the house looking for cracks, holes, and things in the walls needing repair. Nolan pulled me over to her side as she discussed the plumbing with Mr. Townsend.

A few times, Nolan looked completely baffled at a question or comment, and I'd either explain it to her or answer Mr. Townsend's question with what I thought was best. Upstairs in her master bathroom, Milton was foaming at the mouth as she spoke about her vision for the room.

I left the two of them there as Mr. Townsend and I moved on to look in the crawl space for the main house pipes.

I was squatted down beside the house when Pete showed up and joined me.

"How are things looking?"

"Well, for the most part, she needs all new pipes, and after seeing the way the electrical runs in the wall we took down last night, I'm going to say that she is going to need a full rewire. Hence the reason I called you. You might want to take on the job, but then again, you might not."

"Let me take a look. Where is the main junction box?"

I thought about that for a moment. "To be honest, I have no clue." I laughed. "I don't think I have seen one." I told Mr. Townsend I was going back inside.

As Pete and I stepped in, Nolan was coming down the stairs. "Nolan, this is Pete. He works for me and does all my electrical. I asked him to come by and take a look at your wiring to see what he suggests."

She grabbed my arm, squeezing. "Yay!" She let go of my arm to shake his hand but remained close enough to me that her shoulder brushed my arm as she moved. It sent little tingles straight to my groin. Man, I really was hard up, wasn't I?

"Do you know where the electrical panel is?" Pete asked her, and she blinked with the same doe in the headlights look that I was pretty sure I'd had outside.

"I don't remember seeing one."

"Well." He laughed. "There has to be one, so let's take a look, shall we?"

It took us a few minutes to locate it in the laundry room inside a small cupboard. One look inside, and Pete whistled. "I'm not sure how this is rusted, seeing as it's an interior wall, but it is. You're going to need an entirely new panel; besides, this type of panel went out about twenty years ago. I don't think you can even get breakers for it now."

Nolan rested her forehead against my arm in a defeated move and sighed. "I figured as much. How hard would it be to change it out?"

"It's not hard, just a lot of tedious work. The breakers that they use aren't up to code anymore, so I have little doubt that the wiring is." He winced slightly. "Sorry to say, but you are looking at a total rewire of the house."

She turned to me, one brow hiked in question. I nodded. "I was pretty sure that was going to be his suggestion once I saw the wiring last night."

"Ouch!" She winced.

He winked at her. "I can give you a discount since you're a friend of my boss."

I chuckled. "Anything you can do to help, Pete."

"Yes, any help would be great. I want it done right and safely. How long do you anticipate it taking you?"

He scratched his bearded chin. "Three, four days, probably. I could order the new panel and have it this week. I have to start wiring on the house Brad and I are working on soon, but I could probably blow this out before then."

"Get her job done, and then you can work on the other job."

"Alright," he said and waited for Nolan to respond.

She nodded, chewing her bottom lip as she considered that.

"Okay, I guess that is going to have to work." She frowned. "What do you think I could do while there is no power in the house?"

"We could work on the exterior," I suggested.

She turned to me as Pete's phone rang, and he stepped out of the room to take the call. "We?"

I shrugged. "Unless you'd rather me not help."

She put her hand on my arm. "You don't have to. I don't want to pull you away from your real job."

I couldn't help myself; I reached forward and brushed a lock of brown hair off her cheek. "You aren't pulling me anywhere. I want to help."

Like earlier, leaning forward and brushing my lips with hers felt like the natural thing to do. When she curled her arm around my neck and tugged me closer for another kiss, I didn't fight it.

# CHAPTER ELEVEN

## NOLAN

*I* was a little overwhelmed with everything, especially with the kiss that Brad was giving me. It felt different. It felt good.

We pulled back after the kiss was over and smiled at one another. "Thank you," I told him.

His brow furrowed as he stared back at me. "For what?"

"For everything. For being here, and calling your friends in, and for just helping me with all of this."

He gave me a gentle smile that lit up his eyes. "You're welcome. I'm glad I can help."

"Brad!" Kayley shouted from the other room.

He winked at me before he turned and walked out of the laundry room. "Yeah."

"Chester is here."

"Who is Chester?" I asked as I followed him and came to his side.

"Another friend of mine. You mentioned that you wanted stone in your entry. He does masonry."

I threw my arms around him and hugged him tightly. "You really are my new best friend."

His chuckle vibrated through his chest, and I was tempted to nuzzle my face against his torso. He felt so good to hold on to, but I forced myself to step away.

"Hey, I thought I was your best friend?" Kayley pretended to be hurt.

"You are, but he is too, now."

"Alright, fine," she muttered and then grinned widely as I turned to meet the new guy.

Chester was built like a brick himself and covered in tattoos. Brad made the introductions, and I found myself staring at all the ink on his arms.

"I bet every one of those has a story."

He gave me a smirk as he checked me out, his blue eyes dark. "Yep, they do. Maybe someday, I can share them with you."

Brad put his hand on my shoulder. "Some of those stories might scare you, Nolan." I looked between Brad and Chester for a second. Was there some private conversation going on? Chester shifted back slightly, and then Brad let his hand fall to my lower back as he pointed toward the front entry. "I'll show you where the work will be done."

I glanced at Kayley, who had a brow up. So, I wasn't the only one to notice the possessive movement by Brad. Well, that was interesting. I wasn't sure if it was good, but maybe he knew something about his friend that I didn't.

Once in the entryway, Chester and I discussed my thoughts and his suggestions. Brad remained quiet but right at my side. As we talked, another man came in, and Brad introduced me to Chad.

Brad told him that Milton was upstairs, and Chad made his way up the stairs, curiously checking me out. This time, Brad didn't seem bothered by it and had already returned his attention to Chester.

Chester commented that he would bring over samples next week and could probably get the job done in a few weeks as he was backed up with other jobs. He left as quickly as he came, and Brad seemed to relax once he was gone.

Everyone was working, and I was walking around supervising more than anything else. When Mr. Townsend explained what needed to be done, I knew that, while expensive, it was vital and would add equity and soundness to the home. He would start on Wednesday, and I told him I'd get a key over to him since I'd be working.

Chad and Milton were up in my bathroom, tearing out the old fixtures. I watched in awe as the bathroom was dismantled. I felt a little sad that I hadn't gotten to help, but I was glad that I had people here to assist me get so much done.

It was almost one when Kayley's parents arrived, and with them were two children. I knew that they were Brad's kids, as they both had his dark-brown hair and cinnamon-colored eyes.

Tonya stared at me for a moment as if surprised to see me. "Hi, Ms. Nickels. I didn't know we were coming to see you."

"Hi, Tonya. Welcome to my new home."

"Wow, I can't believe my dad is helping you."

"He is," I replied. "I heard you were at the soccer game yesterday. You have any interest in playing?"

She looked away nervously. "I'm not very good."

I put my hand on her shoulder. "You know, when I first started, I was in ninth grade, and I was horrible. The coach never let me on the field, but I kept practicing, and I got better. I was determined to prove to myself and my coach that I could do it. By tenth grade, I was in the starting line of the varsity squad."

"Really?" Her pretty brown eyes lit up.

"True story. I could help you, give you some pointers on what to practice."

"Would you do that?"

"Absolutely."

"I'd love that. I love soccer, but I have never been good."

"Well, we will figure out a time that I can help you."

"Thank you," she said as Brad suddenly appeared at my side.

"Thank you for what?" he asked his daughter.

"Ms. Nickels is going to help me get better at soccer."

"She is, is she?"

Tonya nodded excitedly.

"Alright, well, that's not happening today. Go help Grandma get the food out for everyone."

"Okay." She hustled around us and out to the back porch.

"You don't have to do that," he said once she was out of earshot.

"I want to. I remember wanting to play so badly when I was younger but not having the talent for it. Some people are born with the talent for sports. Others have to work hard to achieve it. I had to bust my ass—and then some."

"Did you play any other sports?" he asked as we went back to join the others.

"Not competitively. I tried out gymnastics but kept getting hurt. Wasn't a big fan of tennis either. Found that I sunk better than floated in swimming, and my hips didn't move with the right beat in dancing."

He laughed. "So soccer it was."

"Yeah, I was always fast, and I'm normally not aggressive, but on the field, I was."

"Yeah, Tonya is not aggressive at all."

"We'll see," I told him as we joined the others. Over lunch, Brad sat with his kids and listened to the tales of the circus. From time to time, we would catch each other's eyes, but his attention was on his kids for the most part. He was a good father.

I sighed as I compared our two little families. Well, his big family, and my little one. Yes, my parents were still around, but they weren't all that involved in anything other than their grandchildren. We didn't have weekly family meals, and I didn't talk to my parents all the time like I knew Kayley and her siblings did.

I envied them that. I had a brother, but he was killed in a boat accident when he was twenty-two. They were drinking and water skiing, and it was not a good mix.

Rick had two sisters, but I had never been very close with them. They were more similar to Riley, Kayley's younger sister, where they wanted to go out all the time and party. I preferred to come home, shower, get into cozy clothes, cook a nice meal, and relax with my girls.

I missed my girls, but it was nice to have a little break. My girls were a lot of work, especially Emmy, my younger one. She was on the spectrum, and it was a constant challenge to make sure she wasn't overstimulating herself. Plus, having her here with all this mess and activity would have put her OCD into overdrive.

I knew they were safe, especially Emmy. Lauren was easier to deal with when she wasn't acting like her father. I swear she was his little mini. She even glared at me the same way he did from time to time. I didn't get a chance to chat with them last night but had told the girls that I would call them later tonight.

As I watched Brad with his kids, I wondered if my girls would get along with them. I knew they would meet eventually, and I hoped they got along, but the kids were at that odd age. They were finding themselves, and with Emmy being autistic, it was hard for some kids to accept her—something she didn't always understand.

After lunch was over, Milton and Chad took off, stating they had other plans. Cameron left to nap because he was on the night shift tonight, and Kayley said she had errands to run. Pete had left before Mr. and Mrs. Young had arrived.

I expected Brad to leave too, but after packing his kids back up in his parents' SUV, he came back into the house. "Don't you want to go hang out with your kids?"

"I will in a little while. I wanted to make sure we had all this cleaned up."

"I can take care of that."

"Don't be silly. It was a whirlwind in here today with everyone. I'll help get it cleaned up, and then—"

"Then what?"

He glanced around quickly as if he were nervous to say something. I held my tongue, waiting for him to go ahead.

"Well, I was going to ask you if you wanted to come to my parents' house tonight for dinner."

"That is nice of you, Brad, but I think I might take a long hot shower and call my girls. I also have some papers to grade."

"Oh." He nodded, looking a little disappointed.

"Maybe next weekend, if the invitation still stands."

"Of course." His smile returned.

For the next hour, we cleaned up, and I made a list of little jobs I could do during the week. One of those jobs was picking out paint for the walls. I hadn't realized that Cameron and Kayley had done so much spackling. Most of the walls were ready to be painted already, although I wouldn't do that until the electricity was done in case Pete had to cut into walls.

I looked around my house as I closed windows and turned off lights, and felt this enormous amount of emotion bubble up in my chest that made me blink away tears. I couldn't believe how much had gotten done today, and I couldn't wait to see what was accomplished next week.

I was coming down the stairs as I said as much to Brad. "Originally, I was hoping to be sleeping in here already."

"Better to wait for the plumbing and electrical work to be finished."

I stopped on the bottom step, and Brad approached me. "Yeah, you're right." The two of us locked gazes. "Thank you for everything, Brad."

"You're welcome, Nolan. I'm glad I could help."

We continued to watch one another, and I put my hand on his chest. "May I kiss you, Brad?"

He shuffled forward slightly. "I'd like that, Nolan."

Brad wrapped me in his strong arms and brought my body to his as our mouths found one another. The kiss was so intense that my toes curled in my sneakers, and I clung to him, not wanting it to end. Within a few seconds, our kisses became more intense, and his hands roamed over my back, one of them cupping my bottom, and I whimpered.

I broke the kiss, leaning my forehead to his. "We need to stop, or I'm going to throw you to the stairs and have my wicked way with you."

He chuckled slightly. "I'm almost ready for you to do that."

I lifted my gaze to him. "Almost? You mean if I keep kissing you, you might let me?"

He brushed his lips over my forehead and stepped back, dropping his hands to his sides. "Not today, but you keep it up, and you might wear down my defenses."

I grinned as I grabbed a fistful of his shirt and yanked him back to me to wrap my arms around his neck. A moment later, I hopped up and wrapped my legs around his waist, and he groaned.

"Nolan, you're killing me here."

I began to kiss his neck, coming up to his ear and whispering, "But what a way to die."

His laughter vibrated through me as I nipped at his earlobe. He moved, shifting our bodies so my back was against the wall, and then he grabbed my face and held it in front of him. I was waiting for him to tell me to stop, to behave, but the look in his eyes said something else entirely different.

His mouth slammed over mine, and I giggled to myself as I realized I had broken through his resistance. Score one for the home team!

# CHAPTER TWELVE

## BRADLEY

This woman had been driving me nuts all day, and she hadn't done anything but be herself. She hadn't tried to entice me, but every look she gave me, every touch in passing, made the small flame in my gut grow into an inferno.

By the time everyone left, I was ready to throw her over my shoulder and bring her home with me. I had hoped that she would have dinner with my family tonight, but she had said no. The thought of walking away from her without kissing her again felt so damn wrong.

Holding her close to me, hearing the soft sounds she made as I kissed her and touched her body felt so damn right. She didn't push me, didn't encourage me to go further than kiss her, but I was pretty quickly coming to the point that I didn't want to stop.

That's why I did. We were both filthy, and again, I didn't have a condom with me, or a bed to lay her beautiful body down on. I rested my forehead to hers, trying to calm my libido.

She seemed as content as I was to stay like that for a few moments in silence. Finally, I lifted my gaze to her, and she gave me a sweet but rather sexy smile as she tilted her head. "Did I make it into the top five yet?"

I laughed. "Lady, I'm pretty sure you are in the top spot for the best kisser."

"Top spot, huh?" She grinned playfully. "I wonder what spot I'd rank for sex."

I closed my eyes. "You're killing me here."

"I'd say sorry, but I'm not."

"You know, if you had a shower and a bed in this place, I might be in trouble."

She sighed and let her head lean back against the wall. "Alas, I do not, and we both *do* need a shower."

"That we do." I stepped back, helping her get her balance back on her feet but not removing my hands from her waist. "You sure you don't want to join us for dinner?"

"Is there going to be a shower and a bed there?"

I chuckled. "No, I just thought you might want to relax with the family."

Her face shuttered slightly, and her smile seemed almost forced. "Thank you. I do appreciate that, and I will take you up on it another time. I'm tired and sore. I really want that hot shower and to kick back and relax."

"That's right. You need to grade your papers, too."

"Yep, that I do."

"Alright, then I'll let you go and do that." It was probably for the best.

I walked her out to her car, and then kissed her once again slowly. "Have a good night."

"You, too. Tell everyone I said hello."

"Will do." I pulled out of the driveway as she turned the headlights of her car on and then drove away.

On the way home, I was at a traffic light waiting for it to turn green when my gaze fell on the pharmacy on the corner. Before I could talk myself out of it, I pulled into the parking lot.

For a second, I stared at the side of the building. Was I really going to buy condoms? Jesus, I hadn't been nervous about buying them since I was seventeen.

I yanked the key from the ignition and got out, shaking my head. I was a grown man with two kids. Buying condoms should be a regular practice for me. That didn't keep me from searching the parking lot to see if I recognized anyone's car or scanning the aisles as I made my way back to the personal protection shelves.

I stood there, staring at all the boxes. Holy shit! What happened to good old regular condoms? There must have been twenty different kinds staring back at me. My gaze landed on the Mega Big Boy Condoms for penises eight inches in length. Are you shitting me?

I shook my head and continued scanning. Fantasy Rainbow. No. Bareskin Studded Condoms—why would you want them studded? Bareback? I thought that was when you went without a condom. Wet & Wild—um, no. Condoms with lubricant, spermicide, and even aloe. Seriously? Who put aloe on their penis?

I picked up a box blindly as I felt someone coming my way. I forced myself not to look and hoped like hell my cheeks weren't as red as they felt. A male hand reached out and grabbed a box that said Trojan Natural Lamb Condoms. The hand paused in front of me. The front of the box facing at me, and I glanced into the face of the man holding and did a double take.

"These should work better for you," Henley, one of my younger brothers, said as he tried to hold back a smirk.

I shook my head as I took the box from him. "Thanks. I didn't realize that there were so many kinds now."

He took the box from my hand and laughed. "Magnum, huh?"

"I just grabbed a box," I muttered.

"Yeah, wishful thinking," he said as he put it back and waved a hand at the shelves. "Yeah, times have changed. You need help with anything else? Want some KY massage oil or lubricant? I'd hate for you to pick up the self-warming without knowing."

I shook my head, slightly mortified as I turned away. "No."

"You're welcome. See you at dinner," Henley called out as I walked away. "Or should I tell the family you have other plans?"

"I'll be there," I growled. I had no doubt that by the time dessert was on the table, everyone would know that I'd bought this box of twelve.

I paid for the purchase and carried the little bag out to my truck, shaking my head at my luck. At least it wasn't Huntley. Jesus, he would have sent out a mass text to the family and all of his friends.

At home, I took a shower and plugged my laptop in to charge. I brought up the design for her kitchen and printed it out. I could give it to Kayley to take home to Nolan.

Before I left, I stared at the box that I had bought, and then I tore it open and pulled out a condom and slipped it into my wallet. Not that I was going to have sex tonight, but at least I would be ready if the opportunity did come up in the future.

I was in traffic, heading to my parents' when I saw Kayley turn from the direction of her house. In the passenger seat was Becky, her ward. Cam was working, so Nolan would be home alone.

At the last second, I made the turn toward Kayley's house. I could drop off the rendering for her myself and still get to dinner on time. At Kayley's home, I paused before I got out of the truck. Maybe I should have just given it to Kay and let it go at that. What would Nolan think of me showing up here uninvited?

I didn't want to think about it. I was here, and I might as well drop it off. It would take two minutes tops.

I knocked on the front door and waited. A few moments later, the door opened. Nolan stood there with a towel wrapped around her head and another one around her body. "Brad, everything okay?"

I forced myself not to devour her with my eyes as I thrust the rendering out to her. "I thought you might want this so you can order the cabinets."

She stared at it and then me. "Is that the only reason you came over here?"

"Yes."

She smirked and reached for the rendering, only she reached past the paper and grabbed my arm, tugging me forward. "I think you came for a different reason."

"No, I was going to give it to Kayley, but I was driving by, so I decided to stop and give it to you so she wouldn't lose it."

I stood in the foyer now, and Nolan studied me carefully. "You showered."

"Looks like you did too."

"There is a bed here."

"Probably a couple," I responded.

She pushed the door closed with one hand. "You realize that you are here alone with me now. Both of us are clean and in a house with multiple beds."

"Yes," I replied dumbly.

"What if my towel dropped to the floor right now? Would you bend down to pick it up for me?"

I swallowed. "Yes."

With slow, purposeful hands, she took the edges of her towel and unhooked them. She paused for a second, staring up at me as she let it go, and it slithered to the ground.

Our eyes were still locked as she whispered, "Would you pick that up for me, Brad?"

I went to my knees, my eyes still stuck on hers until I touched the material of the towel, then they began to fall. I let them drift down her chest to her pert breasts, over her toned stomach, to her hips. I could imagine spanning my hands over those hips, pulling her to me. My gaze dropped further to the juncture of her legs, where her brown curls were neatly trimmed and hiding the sensitive flesh.

Nolan waited as I continued to follow her legs to the ground and noted her pretty light-blue toenails. Her name might be masculine, and she might be into sports and construction, but this woman was one hundred and fifty percent feminine.

I slowly let my gaze drift back up her body as my breathing grew ragged, and I began to get to my feet. I was halfway up when I dropped the towel from my grasp and instead put my hands on the soft skin of her waist. I ran them up the sides of her body, my thumbs brushing her perfect breasts, and I leaned forward and kissed her neck, then lower, then on her collarbone before I kissed a path lower. Slowly, I moved until I was about to suckle her nipple. I paused for just a fraction of a second, and her hand gently brushed over the back of my head, pulling me forward.

I latched on to her breast, palming the other one and squeezing gently. I went back to my knees as I lavished her other one and then her stomach. My hands held her hips firmly as I licked and kissed over the firm flesh of her belly.

I wanted to go lower, to taste her, but I wasn't sure she would like that. Instead, I ran my hands down the lengths of her legs, then came back up, curling my fingers around the backs of her thighs and cupping her ass as I reached it.

I kissed her lower stomach, looking up at her. She was watching me. Her lips parted, her eyes slightly glazed as I brushed my lips over her soft hair. I went lower, smelling her arousal and feeling like I was going to lose my cool before it even got started.

As if sensing that I was holding myself tightly, she pulled my arm up. "Come to my room."

I wasn't able to speak with the scent of her still in my nostrils. Instead, I followed her as she led me naked to the guest room. Behind her, I watched her butt cheeks wiggle with each step, dying to run my hands over them again.

Inside the bedroom, she let go of my hand and sat on the edge of the bed. After a few seconds, Nolan shifted her legs wider, and I almost wept. My legs shook as I dropped to my knees again, but before I lost myself in her sensitive flesh, I took hold of her face and kissed her more deeply than we had previously.

A few moments later, I was working my way back down her body, and as I began to kiss her hip bones, she lay back on the bed, opening herself up for me. I got lost in her skin and her taste—her soft moans adding to my pleasure as if she were stroking me already.

As it was, my pants were extremely tight, and I eased back the buckle and released the pressure by unzipping my jeans. I had barely done that when Nolan began to squirm under my mouth, and I worked faster. She shattered around me with only my mouth on her, and I wondered what she would feel like when she did that while I was inside of her.

She had barely finished her orgasm when she pushed for me to stand, and she sat up again. Her hands went right to my jeans, and she began to tug at them to get them off.

I pushed her hands off as I chuckled. "Slow down, woman."

"No," she growled at me but let her hands drop to her lap. I pulled my jeans, shoes, and socks off, and then my t-shirt. Her gaze ran over my chest, and her hands were right there too. After a few seconds of touching my chest, she snagged the waistband of my boxers and pulled them down.

She made a moaning noise, and I hoped that was a good thing as she stared at my erection. Before my boxers even hit the floor, she had wrapped her hand around my shaft, and her tongue came out to lick the head.

In that one moment, I felt like I had died and gone to heaven.

# CHAPTER THIRTEEN

## NOLAN

This man was perfect. His touch was perfect. The way his work-calloused hands brushed so lightly over my skin was perfect, and oh my god, his mouth was beyond perfection.

I wanted to taste the man. I needed to taste him. He only let me for a few moments, and I understood why. He hadn't been with anyone in a long time. I felt privileged to be his first since his wife, and I was determined to help him enjoy it so that he would come back for more.

He stepped out of his pants, and I scooted farther up on the bed. He was about to climb on when he returned to his pants for something, and I realized he had brought a condom with him. He didn't need it, but I wasn't going to tell him that.

Brad had the package in his hands, and I kept quiet. I could see the internal debate he was having and didn't want to intrude. His gaze skimmed over my body, and finally, I held my hand out to him. "Come to me, Brad."

He put his knee to the mattress and laced his fingers with mine before he brought our bodies together. For a few minutes, I allowed him to explore my body again. I was anxious to have him deep within me, but I didn't want to rush him, not this time.

Finally, I pushed him to his back and peeled the condom out of his fisted hand. On my knees beside him, I tore it open, keeping his gaze locked with mine. I smiled at him reassuringly as I reached forward and began to unroll the condom. He watched my every move, and when he started to shift to sit up, I held him down and straddled his legs.

"Jesus," he moaned as I ground my sensitive flesh over his. His hands came to my hips, and I rolled them to line him up. I slowly pushed back, feeling him fill me the further I went. He moaned again, his fingers tightening on my hips, and I paused.

He finally opened his eyes, and I leaned forward and kissed him, then placed kisses on his chest before I began to move over him. Within a few minutes, his breathing accelerated; his neck corded as if he were holding himself back, and I picked up the pace. I knew he wouldn't last much longer, and I wanted to hit that goal alongside him.

He hit the goal line just a moment before I did, and when I finally crossed it, he practically shouted at the intensity of our coming together. I collapsed onto his chest, listening to his thunderous heart hammering in his chest and loving the hair that covered the skin there. My god, did I need that.

I remained where I was until his heartbeat was back to normal. His hand was drifting in slow circles over my back as I snuggled against him and sighed happily.

"I'm sorry that wasn't longer," he finally spoke huskily.

I shifted so I could see his face. "Do you see me complaining? I do believe I am lying here happily sated from two incredible orgasms."

He chuckled and cupped my cheek. "I'm glad you are."

"Was that okay for you?"

He barked out a laugh and then winced as his sensitive shaft was still firmly encompassed within me. I lifted my hips and rolled to the side, where he followed me.

"That was more than okay." He studied my face and then kissed me tenderly. "Now, I wish I had more than one condom with me."

"You don't need one."

His frow furrowed for a second. "I don't think we should be taking any chances."

"Brad, I can't get pregnant if that's what you are worried about. I had a partial hysterectomy a few years ago. And if you are worried about some disease, well, I haven't had sex with anyone in two years, so I'm pretty sure I'm STD-free."

"You tell me that now?" He laughed. "If I had known that, I might have taken you up against the wall earlier today."

I laughed with him. "We were rather dirty."

He leaned down and kissed me. "A little bit of dirt never hurt anyone, did it?"

I shook my head as a notification came from the floor, and Brad sighed. "Text message. It's probably one of my brothers wondering where I am."

"Well, then you better get going."

"Yeah, I should." Before he got up, he kissed me again, and then I told him to feel free to use the bathroom before he dressed. I had my robe on when he returned with his jeans back in place and I watched as he slipped his t-shirt on, then his socks and shoes.

I walked him to the door. "I'm sorry I have to leave. This isn't me. I don't just have sex and run away."

"I know you don't, Brad, but you have places to be, and I have things to do. I'm glad you came over. Now go enjoy dinner with your family, and I'll see you later."

"Can I call you later tonight?"

"I have work to do," I told him. "I'll talk to you tomorrow. Go have fun."

"Fine." He sighed, but he was smiling as he did so. "I'll see you later."

After one final kiss, I watched him walk down the front steps to his truck. I closed the door after a last wave and leaned my forehead against the door.

"Well, damn," I muttered to myself. I had wanted to have sex with Brad as a stress reliever. A wham-bam kind of thing, but it had felt like more than that. I didn't need or want more than that.

I had seen it in his eyes as he'd said goodbye. He had feelings for me—or he could have feelings for me. I didn't want him to have feelings for me, and I sure didn't want to have feelings for him. My life was way too busy to add in a man who had two children.

I pushed off the door and went back to my room to get dressed, call the girls, and then work on my papers.

~

School was busy the next day, and then we had soccer practice. By the time I got out of there, I was dragging. Unfortunately, I still had things to do for school, which ended up being an early night.

Tuesday after work, I drove to Summersville, which was an hour away, to shop in the larger hardware store. I knew what color paint I wanted for my bedroom but needed swatches for the house's other rooms.

I heard my phone announce a few notifications, but I was in my element and focused on what I was doing. Or more like, I was in planning mode as I moved slowly down each aisle, looking for things that I would need to complete my projects.

I had about a hundred and fifty thousand to put into restoring the house. That was after selling my home in New York for a significant profit and getting this new one for a bargain, plus tapping into my savings. A good thirty grand was going to the plumbing job. Another thirty to my kitchen and about ten thousand for the rewire, plus or minus a grand. Right there was seventy thousand dollars for those three projects alone. That didn't include the bathroom remodels, the new washer and dryer, replacing the porch that ran around the house on three sides, the stone wall in the entryway, new lighting fixtures, or floor restoration.

Oh my god! What was the floor going to cost? I rubbed my temples for a few moments. Maybe I should do some research on wood floor restoration and do it myself. It wasn't anything I had ever wanted to do before, but if it would save me some money, then maybe.

I would have to ask Brad if he knew anyone who restored old wood floors. I'm sure he knew someone. He knew practically everyone. In a weekend, he had almost sourced out my entire house—except my garage. Damn. I forgot about building the garage.

I pulled out my phone and quickly searched for the average cost of building a two-car garage. The estimate was twenty to thirty thousand. I winced. Maybe I would put up a one car garage instead. The highest estimate on that was only fifteen thousand.

While I had my phone in hand, I checked to see what messages I had. I had one from Kayley asking if I was going to be home for dinner. I replied that I wouldn't.

I had a second message from one of my soccer player's parents asking about an upcoming game. I replied to that one too.

Lauren sent me a picture of her and Emmy doing a puzzle. I replied that I loved it and told her I'd talk to her at eight tonight.

Then I stared at the message from Brad. *You working on your house tonight?*

I responded, *Yes, but not physically. I'm in Summersville running errands.*

Kayley had sent me a reply. *Brad keeping you busy tonight?*

I took a picture of my loaded cart. *No Brad here. Shopping keeping me busy.*

Brad's response arrived. *You should have told me you were going out there. I could have saved you some money with my discounts.*

I stared at the message and pursed my lips. It was kind for Brad to offer such a thing, but I didn't want to be indebted to him. He had already done so much to help me. I finally wrote back. *Oh, that would have been nice. Next time! Have a great night!*

I sent the message and then tossed my phone back into the small purse I carried and started down another aisle. I was in the store for over two hours, and when I left, I'd spent over six hundred dollars. I loaded it all into my car, and my stomach rumbled.

With a glance at the clock on my phone, I realized that it was almost eight. I needed to get something to eat and then do a video chat with my girls. Then I could drive home, unload the car at the house, and get a good night's rest at Kayley's.

I ran through a drive-thru, picking up a greasy burger and fries, and then parked and video called Lauren's phone.

"Hey, Mom!" Lauren said as she answered.

"Hey, sweetheart, how are you?"

"I'm good. How is the house?"

"It is coming right along. If all goes well, you guys will probably be able to come down as soon as school ends."

"I thought we weren't coming down until the middle of the summer?"

"Yeah, well, I have a bunch of people working on the house with me, and with this team, I think it is going to get done in record time."

"That's cool!"

"Hey, I need you to ask Grandma to do me a favor."

Lauren pulled the phone away from her face. "Grandma! Mom needs to talk to you."

A moment later, my mom's face filled the screen. "How are you, honey? How is the house?"

"I'm tired but good, and the house is moving along. It's going to go pretty fast, I think, but I need some help from you guys back home."

"Alright, what can we do?"

"Can you take the girls to the hardware store to look at paint swatches? Have them pick out three different colors, and I'll see which one works best for their room."

"We can do that this weekend."

"Great, then you can mail them down to me."

"We get to pick out our paint?" I heard Emmy ask in the background. My mother handed the phone back to Lauren after a quick goodbye.

"You do."

"Can we paint it too?" Emmy asked.

"Well, I think it might be best if I surprise you with one of the colors you choose. Wouldn't that be fun?"

"Yeah, I guess." She didn't seem quite as enthusiastic. I had tried to paint something with her before, but her OCD was a little intense as the paint went on the wall, and she had to keep rolling the same spot over and over again to make sure it was right.

I turned the conversation away from the house and asked how each of them was doing. "Are you guys taking your medicine?"

"Emmy didn't want to take hers this morning, but I talked her into it," Lauren said.

"And you? Are you taking your medicine?"

"Yeah, Mom, I am."

"Okay, good. Are you having any problems with it?"

"Nope, and I take my blood pressure every morning and every night and see the nurse after lunch for her to take it too."

"Alright. That's good." I stared at my daughter's sweet face, and then Emmy pushed to get into the screen.

"I love you guys and miss you two so much."

"We miss you too," Lauren said as Emmy smiled widely.

We talked for a couple more minutes, and then we said goodbye. As I hung up the phone, I blinked back a few tears. I hated being away from my kids, but I was building a new life for us. These last couple of years had been rough with Emmy's spectrum diagnosis, Lauren's heart defect, and my divorce. Then add in the job change and moving, and it was almost overwhelming.

It was one of the reasons I was working so hard to give us a new life, a new place to start in a stress-free environment where the girls' friends didn't ask a million questions and make fun of the girls because they couldn't do certain things. It was also why I didn't want to get involved with anyone emotionally.

The girls had already had one man walk out of their lives; they didn't need another.

# CHAPTER FOURTEEN

## BRADLEY

*I* had three messages on my phone from people checking in on me. I didn't answer any of them. Instead, I drove to my parents. They probably started dinner without me, and that was fine.

When I got there, everyone was around the table, and a few people called out hello, but no one looked at me funny or made a joke about me not being here on time. My eyes strayed to Henley, and he nodded.

So he hadn't told anyone about earlier today. Why? Tonya gave me a hug as I made my way around the table, and then bowls and platters were passed toward me to fill my plate. My father leaned closer, and I thought, well, here it comes. "You get that problem fixed?"

"Problem?" I echoed back.

Henley spoke up. "Yeah, I told them you'd texted me before dinner that you'd be late because you had a little problem to handle."

"Uh, yeah, I did. Nothing major, just something that needed my attention for a few minutes."

"Well." My dad grinned. "That's good."

I peered around the table quickly, but no one else seemed to be interested in why I was late. I hadn't expected that. I was closing my mouth around a forkful of roast beef when Kayley caught my eye and gave me a conspiratorial grin. The laughter in her eyes told me she knew precisely what I had to work on.

I forced myself not to think about it anymore and attempted to get on board with the conversation around the table. Every once in a while, a memory of Nolan would show up in my mind, and I would have to wrestle it back into hiding. I didn't need my hormones to jack up now as I sat at the table with my family.

Hunt eventually brought up Nolan as he asked Kayley, "How are things going at the Millstone house? I heard that your friend was gutting it."

"She is, and Brad is helping her." Kayley grinned my way, lacing her fingers together as she propped her elbows on the table and then resting her chin on them as if she were an angel or something.

"You're working on the house?" Wes asked as he peeked around his daughter Marisol. "I thought you were in a full construction of a new house right now."

"I am. I'm only helping out."

"Helping out by sharing all his laborers," my father added.

Wes nodded as if he approved.

"I haven't met your friend, Kayley," Roxanne said. "When do I get the pleasure?"

Kayley glanced my way and then smiled at Roxanne. "She'll be here for the Memorial Day picnic."

"Oh, good! I look forward to meeting her."

Memorial Day was a few weeks away, and I wondered where my relationship with Nolan would be then. Maybe we'd have built something solid by then, and we could let the family know. Although how did you build something that was supposed to last a lifetime in only a couple of weeks?

I glanced at Henley, Wes, and Hunt and thought about their relationship. They had fallen in love in days or weeks, and they were all happy.

For the first time in years, I craved that feeling. I hadn't felt loved like that in many years. Maybe since shortly after Tyler was born. God, had it been almost ten years since I felt emotionally and physically close to another person? I stared at my plate, wondering how so much time could have gone by without feeling what I had shared with Nolan earlier today.

"You okay?" Riley asked from beside me.

"Yeah, I'm fine. Just thinking about something." I put my hand on her back and rubbed it for a moment as I sat back in my seat and stared at my family. Cameron wasn't here, but everyone else was, and I realized that for the last several years, I had been hiding from them all, hiding my loneliness behind my work and kids.

I wanted what they had. I wanted someone to love, to be with, to grow old with, and holy crap. I wanted it with Nolan. Suddenly I couldn't hold the words back. "I slept with Nolan today."

Conversation at the table halted, forks scraped over plates like a needle on a vinyl record, and there was a gasp or two.

"Um, kids," Wes immediately began after he cleared his throat. I wanted to face-plant myself into my plate. "Why don't you go out to the barn and feed the horses?"

Marisol was already scooting out of her seat, not caring in the least about the conversation at the table. Tyler was right behind her, but Tonya eyed me carefully as she slipped out of her chair. I was going to have to explain this to her later. She was old enough to understand some of what I'd just said. I tried to smile at her, but it was probably more of a grimace.

The moment the back door closed, Riley spun on me. "You actually had sex with her? Like in bed, and not by yourself as you fantasized over her."

"Riley!" my mother exclaimed as a few people laughed.

"Is this what you needed to fix today?" my father asked seriously.

"Yeah" I told him. My face was burning with embarrassment, but I had brought it on myself.

My father's serious face broke into happiness, and he put his hand on my shoulder and squeezed. "About time you got back out there, Brad. I'd been hoping you'd find someone for ages."

"Yeah, man," Hunt said. "It's about damn time."

Everyone was grinning at me as I looked around the table. My gaze paused on Kayley as she spoke. "I told you that you'd like her."

"Yeah, I guess you were right. I do."

She winked at me, and Riley leaned closer and whispered, "Was it as good as you remembered?"

"Better," I replied with a grin as she giggled, and Ethan shook his head at her.

"Now that you all know that—" Henley smirked my way, and I put my hand up.

"You don't have to tell that story."

"Oh, yes! Yes, I do," he said as he chuckled loudly, and everyone cheered him on to continue with a story that they all knew would embarrass my ass.

I hung my head as he started. "I was at the pharmacy picking up something for the firehouse, and I saw Brad standing in the middle of the aisle looking dumbfounded."

"At what?" Wes asked.

"At the condom selection," Henley replied, and everyone at the table broke up laughing—even my parents.

"Hey, last time I wore that kind of protection, there were like five choices. There were four shelves full of them now. I was confused."

"Did you help him decide?" Daniella asked.

"Yeah." Hen grinned. "I handed him a box of Rainbow Fantasies in extra magnum size."

The table roared with laughter again, and I shook my head. "You did not!" I said with a chuckle. "Yes, he did help me out, and I'm glad that is over."

Daniella was giggling but then got serious. "Hey, I know there are a lot of them out on the market. I had to research them for a book I was writing, and I started clicking on them to see more about them."

"Needless to say," Hunt stepped in, "we have quite an assortment to choose from."

"Hey, those are for research purposes," she scolded him playfully.

"My kind of research," Charlotte added with a giggle.

A comical conversation went on for a little while over the various types of condoms. As the table was being cleared, my mother came to my side. "You might want to go talk with your daughter. I think she was a little concerned with your announcement."

"Yeah, I guess you're right," I told her. She kissed the top of my head and carried the plates to the kitchen sink.

I excused myself from the table and made my way out to the barn. Tyler and Marisol were pouring feed, and Tonya was standing at the side of the paddock, looking perturbed.

I joined her, staring over the land behind my parents' house. "What's on your mind?"

"Do you like Ms. Nickels?"

"I do."

"When you said you slept with her, did that mean—"

"Mean what?" I asked after a few seconds of her hesitation.

"Does that mean you had sex with her?" Her cheeks grew slightly pink.

I inhaled and exhaled loudly. "Yeah, that's what I meant. I forget how grown-up you are."

"I thought you were only supposed to have sex with people when you loved them."

"Hmm," I responded and thought for a moment. "That's a complicated answer, Tonya."

"So, I can go out and have sex with anyone, and it's okay?"

I turned and looked down at her. "No, that is *not* okay. You are way too young to be thinking about having sex with anyone." I shook my head. "Look, there is a difference in having sex when you are a teenager or young adult and when you are my age."

"What's the difference?"

Jesus, what was the difference? How did I explain this to my daughter? "Once you are an adult, you'll be able to decide who you share your body with and who you don't. It's a complicated answer, but yes, you are supposed to love someone before you have sex with them."

"Do you love Ms. Nickels?"

"Honestly?"

She nodded.

"No, I don't know her well enough to love her, but I do like her."

"Is she going to be our new mom?"

"Whoa, that's not even a consideration right now. Nolan and I are getting to know one another, and at our age, sex is part of the process. I know that doesn't make sense, but I do like Nolan, and—" I paused. Did I admit this to my daughter? Yeah, I think she needed to know. "And Nolan is the first woman I have been with since your mother. Your mom has been gone a long time, and it wasn't until I met Nolan that I even wanted to move forward."

Tonya was only six when her mother passed, and while she had a few memories of her, they'd been dulled with time. "Do you think Mom would mind?"

"Mind me moving on? No, she wanted me to. She told me she wanted me to move on."

"She did?"

"Yeah, honey. Your mother knew she was dying, and she knew that I still had a lot of life left to live. She wanted me to be happy and find someone else. It's just taken me a very long time to get to that point and to find someone who interested me enough to take a chance."

"Okay."

"I'm sorry that I blurted that out at the table."

She shrugged. "It's okay."

"I am glad that we had this talk, though. You know when you get older, you can talk to me about this stuff too."

She rolled her eyes. "Dad, I am not talking to you about sex and periods and things like that. I have my aunts to ask."

I chuckled. "Alright, then you talk to them, but don't think you can't speak to me too. I'm always here for you."

She wrapped her arms around my waist and hugged me tightly before she dashed off to help the kids finish feeding the horses.

I watched them as I thought back on when Cheryl was alive. Once she found out she had cancer, the chasm that had been between us seemed to fill itself in, and the two of us grew closer than we had been in years. Maybe it was the fear of the unknown, and Cheryl needed the security of what she knew with me. I didn't know, but she did tell me that she said goodbye to the man that she'd fallen for and that her attention would remain on the kids and me until she was gone.

At the funeral, a man had come up to me and given his regards. Cheryl had never told me the name of the man she'd fallen in love with, but she didn't have to. He didn't say anything to me about how he knew my wife, just gave his condolences and moved on, but I knew. I saw it in his eyes—he had the same pain that I did for losing someone he loved.

We had shaken hands, stared at one another as if having a long conversation, and then he nodded briskly and walked away after one last look over his shoulder at her in the casket.

I guess it was time for me to take that last long look myself and let the past go. I deserved a future. I deserved to be loved and happy, and I was ready. Nolan had made me ready.

# CHAPTER FIFTEEN

## NOLAN

The workweek went by all too quickly, and before I knew it, I was letting myself into my new house Friday after work. I was wiped out, but I didn't have time to be since my project was moving by leaps and bounds.

Mr. Townsend had finished the pipes an hour ago after three very long days. Pete was scheduled to be here tomorrow morning to start the wiring. Milton would bring tile samples over to me later this evening, and he'd jump on the bathroom as soon as he could fit me in, probably next week.

What I was looking forward to the most was sleeping in my new house for the first time. Now that I had running water, I could at least use the powder room downstairs. The toilet and sink were old, but they worked.

It wasn't going to be comfortable staying here, but I was prepared. I'd bought a cushy floor mat and a new sleeping bag. I didn't care how uncomfortable it was. I was determined to sleep in my house.

As I waited for Milton to arrive, I carried things into the house from my car. I had also bought a mini-fridge so I could have a couple of things in my place. I was attempting to lift it out of my car when I heard a vehicle pulling up behind me. I assumed it was Milton, but I turned to see it was Brad.

This was the first I'd seen of him since last Sunday. *Please don't let this be awkward*, I thought to myself as I put the mini-fridge back down. Brad and I had spoken via text a couple of times, but not about anything important. Mostly questions about my house and projects.

"Were you going to carry that yourself?" he said as soon as he stepped out of his truck.

"I got it in there," I told him.

He was shaking his head as he approached. "I know you're strong, Nolan, but you're going to hurt yourself trying to carry that around."

I shrugged. Maybe he was right. I didn't think so, but it wasn't worth arguing over. "Well, then I guess I am glad that I have a big strong man here to help me."

He stared at me for a moment as if he was trying to tell if I was being sarcastic. I tossed him a smile and stepped back. It had been sarcastic, but I didn't mean to take my cranky mood out on Brad.

"How are you doing?" he asked.

"It's been a long week, and it's going to be an even longer weekend."

"Kids at school giving you a hard time?" he asked as he hoisted the small fridge and carried it across the lawn.

"No, not more than kids usually do. I just have so much going on, and it's overwhelming."

"Why don't you take a night off then?"

"Because I have too much to get done."

"Where do you want this?" he asked once inside the house.

"Put it in the dining room so that it's not in the way of the kitchen work."

I followed him into the room and watched as he bent down to set the box on the ground. I couldn't help but stare at his backside as he did and suddenly thought of something that might make my mood better.

I averted my eyes before he stood, telling myself I needed to keep my hormones under control. All week, I had been forcing myself not to think about our tryst, but it had been hard not to. I guess that was why I hadn't been too chatty all week.

"You want me to remove it from the box for you?"

I shrugged. "If you want to."

He turned and studied me. "You okay, Nolan? You seem tense."

"I told you, I'm tired." I waved a hand around.

He came to stand in front of me. "Then you should take a night off. What was it that you needed to do tonight?"

"Just a lot of little things, and I wanted to start painting my bedroom. Plus, Milton is coming over with the tile samples."

"What time is Milton coming?"

"About twenty minutes," I replied.

"Okay, how about we wait for Milton, then I'll take you out to dinner. After that, I can help you paint your bedroom if you want."

"Brad, you don't have to do that. I appreciate everything that you have done for me, but you really don't need to keep helping me."

"I want to."

"Why?"

"Why?"

I nodded. "Yes. Why do you want to help?"

He stared at me for a long time. "Do you *not* want my help?"

"I want to know *why* you want to help."

He glanced around the room. "Because I enjoy doing this type of thing, and I also enjoy spending time with you. It's kind of a win-win situation for me."

For a few moments, we studied one another. I really was exhausted, and I could use a night off. "Okay, after Milton comes by, I'll let you take me out to dinner. Then I'll see how I feel after. I might just crash and get up early and start painting tomorrow."

He smiled, and my tension eased a little bit. I didn't admit it to him, but I enjoyed spending time with him too. That's kind of what my problem was. I liked Brad. I'd thought way too much about the man this week. His easygoing nature, the way he was with his kids, the incredible family he had, and the great sex—we can't forget about the sex.

It might not have been a marathon encounter, but we had fit so perfectly together. Even after years with Rick, sex had some-times felt odd, like we were forcing ourselves to endure the act. There was nothing forced while being with Brad.

I helped Brad get the fridge out of the box, and he said we should leave it to sit there for a little while before we plugged it in. I left my purse on top of it to remind me to plug it in when we went for dinner.

Milton was there shortly after that, and we were discussing tile colors when I got a video chat from Lauren.

"Can you excuse me for a moment? I need to take this." Lauren didn't call me unless it was necessary.

"Hey, Lauren, what's going on?"

"Emmy is having a meltdown. Grandma cleaned her room and moved things around."

"You can't calm her down?"

"No." She sighed.

I had stepped into the other room, and I closed the door behind me. "Put her on."

"Okay, hold on. She's in her bedroom."

Lauren carried the phone toward her sister's room. "How are you doing?"

She shrugged. "Okay. School sucked today, and my blood pressure was high, but I'm okay now."

I frowned. "How high?"

She paused and stared at the camera. "Not too high. I know what it needs to stay under, Mom."

"I know you do, Lauren, but I worry since I'm not there."

"It's okay." She resumed her trek, and I heard her opening the door. "Emmy, Mom is on the phone. She wants to talk to you."

Lauren turned the phone around, and Emmy was adjusting stuffed animals on a shelf. My mom knew better than to go in there and move Emmy's things. That was how we'd realized that she was on the spectrum. I had rearranged her room, and she'd had a major meltdown.

"Emmy, sweetheart, talk to mommy."

"I can't. I need to fix this. Grandma put them all wrong."

"Okay, you will get them back."

She spun and yelled at me, "They will never be back the right way. They were perfect, and now they aren't."

"Emmy, you need to calm down."

She shoved Lauren's hand away. "Go away. I need to get this right."

"Emmy, don't push at your sister. You will get the stuffed animals back in place."

Emmy spun and put her face close to the screen. "No! They will never be right again! She wasn't supposed to touch them! I had them perfect!"

"Sweetheart, stop," I said softly. She frowned slightly but stopped talking. "Close your eyes and remember what your stuffed animals looked like. I know you have the picture in your mind of how they were."

She kept staring at me.

"Emmy, do as I say. Close your eyes and picture them." She finally closed her eyes. "Now picture them how they were. Can you see them?"

After a moment, she nodded, and then her eyes popped open, and the angry look was gone. In its place was determination. She turned away from the phone and began to move them around. A moment later, she paused, and I could tell by her profile that she had her eyes closed again. She opened them again and got back to work, this time with a slight smile on her lips.

"Excellent, Emmy. See? You know how they go. You will make them perfect again."

She didn't say anything as all her focus was on her task.

"Emmy, I'll talk to you later. Lauren, can you take the phone to Grandma, please?"

"Yeah," Lauren replied. "I told Grandma yesterday that I would help Emmy clean her room. I knew this was going to happen."

"Thank you, sweetie."

"Grandma, Mom is on the phone." She handed her phone over to my mother, who put it to her ear.

"Mom, it's a video call, not a phone call."

"Oh!" She pulled it away from her ear and stared at the screen. "How are you?"

"I'd be better if you hadn't cleaned Emmy's room."

"It was dusty. She'll get over it."

"Mom, she will get over it, but do you know how much that stresses her out when her room isn't how she wants it? Next time, have Lauren help her clean it. That way, Emmy does it how she wants to. She can clean her room, and she likes to clean, so ask her to do it. Don't go in there and move her things."

"Nolan, you make more out of this than there is."

"Mom! If you move her stuff around, then you are stressing her out. You stress her out, it stresses Lauren out, and then it stresses me out, and I'm four hours away and can't do a damn thing to help."

My mother frowned and shook her head.

"I appreciate that you are watching them, Mom, but please,

just let Emmy clean her room. You know how specific she is. Okay?"

"Fine." She sighed and handed the phone back to Lauren as she muttered something about not understanding this whole spectrum thing.

I hung my head and closed my eyes for a moment, and Lauren walked away with the phone. "I'm sorry you had to deal with that."

"You sure we can't move down with you sooner?"

"Honey, it's going to be a while before we get this house suitable for you guys. If you think her stuffed animals being out of whack was stressful, imagine what a torn apart house would do to her?"

"Yeah, I guess. Just hurry up."

"Sweetheart, you only have a month of school left. After that is over, we'll get you moved down."

"I don't care about school," she muttered as she flopped back on her bed.

"What happened at school today?"

"Nothing."

"You said school sucked, and you were stressed, so what happened?"

She rolled her eyes. "I wasn't able to do something at school today, and a couple of the kids were making fun of me."

Goddamn kids and their stupid mouths! Ugh! "I'm sorry, honey. I know that's rough. I wish I was there to hug you."

She looked so sad as she stared at me. "I wish you were too."

"I promise I will get this house done as quickly as I can and have you guys here before you know it."

"It can't be soon enough."

"I love you, Lauren."

"Love you too, Mom."

"Okay, I need to go. We are picking out tile for my bathroom."

"I wish I was there to help."

"Maybe you can help me pick out tile for your bathroom. Would you like to do that?"

"Like we did with the paint samples?"

"Well, maybe over a video chat."

She smiled. "Yeah, I want to do that."

"Alright, then when we get to your bathroom, not today, Milton and I can show you the choices."

"Who is Milton?"

"The man who is doing my bathroom tile."

"Oh, okay. Is he cute?"

I laughed. "Lauren, why would you care if he is cute?"

"I don't." She grinned mischievously at me. "But maybe you do."

"Well, Milton is a nice man, but not my type."

"Okay, fine," Lauren said dramatically.

"I have to go. I'll talk to you later."

"You know, Mom, someday you are going to find a man you like."

I laughed. "That is not something that I am interested in right now, Lauren. I have to go. I love you, and I will talk to you tomorrow."

"Love you, too."

I hung up and inhaled deeply before releasing it. When I turned around, I found Brad standing in the doorway.

"Is that really something that you are not interested in?"

# CHAPTER SIXTEEN

## BRADLEY

*I* didn't normally eavesdrop, but I was interested in her relationship with her girls. As I stood there, I realized that she didn't speak much about them. In fact, I don't think I even knew their names.

I knew them now, but only because I had come to check on her when I heard her raise her voice. The conversation that I overheard confused me, and I wondered why a child would get so upset because someone had cleaned their room. Both of my kids would have been ecstatic if I had cleaned theirs.

What really caught my attention was the last thing she said about not wanting to find someone. Was that true?

I pushed the door the rest of the way open and stepped inside. "Is that really something that you are not interested in?"

She pursed her lips like she wasn't happy I was there. I guess she had a right to be. Finally, she slipped her phone into her pocket and crossed her arms over her chest. "How long were you listening?"

"I came to check on you when I heard your voice getting louder. It sounded like you were upset."

"I was, but it is none of your business."

"I'm sorry. I was just making sure you were alright."

"I'm fine. Just a small issue at home. I need to get back to Milton." She began to approach, and I stepped aside to let her pass.

She was much different today than she had been last week. Maybe she was just tired, but perhaps there was something else bothering her. As I followed her back to her bathroom, I pondered how I could get her to open up.

She was quiet as she worked with Milton, and I could tell her heart wasn't into what she was doing. She waffled over three different tiles, and finally, Milton suggested she think it over and let him know the next day. I thought that was a great idea.

Obviously, she was exhausted and stressed, and I stepped away from them for a few moments to make a phone call. When I came back, they were finishing up, and I studied her profile. She had circles under her eyes and tiny lines on her forehead that weren't normally there.

After we walked Milton out, she turned to me, and I saw it coming, but I wasn't going to let her back out. "Get your purse, and let's go eat."

"Brad, I'm tired. Like suddenly exhausted."

I cupped her cheek. "I know you are. That's why I already ordered dinner, and we will pick it up and go back to my place. After you eat, you can rest."

"I plan on sleeping here tonight."

"With as tired as you are, I think a good night's sleep in a bed is what you need."

"I've been sleeping in a bed all week, and it hasn't helped."

"Did you have someone there to rub your back?"

Her lips parted in surprised delight. "Oh, you rub backs?"

"I do."

"Okay, you won."

Before I let her walk away, I kissed her once tenderly. She

was dragging her feet but not fighting me as she returned with her purse, and we locked up her house. I led her to my truck and helped her get inside.

I had ordered Italian from my favorite place near my house and stopped to pick it up, leaving her inside the truck as I did so. She was yawning when I came back.

"You need to get some sleep. Have you not been sleeping at night?"

"I've been at the house late every night and then grading papers. I guess I just wore myself out."

"Sounds like it."

She seemed to perk up a bit as she looked around at my house, and I gathered plates and utensils for us. "Would you like a glass of wine?"

"Yes, I would love one."

I uncorked one of my favorite Shirazes and poured us each a glass before we took a seat at the table. She put food on her plate but then pushed it around as she stared off to the side. I followed her line of vision to a picture of Cheryl and the kids.

"That's Cheryl," I said as if she wouldn't have already guessed.

She nodded. "I bet she was a good wife and mother, huh?"

"She was a better mother than wife," I finally replied, and that got her attention.

"Why wasn't she a good wife?"

I put a forkful of pasta in my mouth and chewed. Had she forgotten that I had already told her that Cheryl had cheated on me?

"Do you remember me telling you about her wanting a divorce to be with someone else?"

She frowned. "Yeah, I do. Any idea what happened in your relationship for that to happen?"

I shrugged and then wiped my mouth. "We wanted different things. I wanted a family life. I wanted to come home to my family and relax. She wanted to go out and have fun. I let her, and I guess she started having too much fun because she started to find other things that she wanted to do that didn't include me, or a lot of times the kids."

"Like what things?"

I hesitated and then finally replied, "Like wine tasting class and ballroom dancing lessons."

"Do you think that's what the other man wanted her to do?"

I nodded and resumed eating for a moment. "I assume it was his influence on her."

"Why do you think she stayed with you after she found out she had cancer? If she loved this other man, why didn't she didn't spend her last days with him?"

"I have wondered that myself. I guess she realized that I was a better provider and protector than the other man, or she didn't love him all that much after all."

"Wow," Nolan stated softly.

"When she finally confirmed that she was seeing another man, I told her I wanted a divorce. I wasn't going to hold her back from having the life that she wanted—even though it hurt. I guess once we grew further apart, I realized that it wasn't going to work, and I don't think I loved her as much as I thought I did. In fact, I know I didn't."

"If you didn't love her that much, why have you not dated other women?"

"Who said I didn't?"

"Oh, I guess I just assumed."

"I have dated a few women, but I wasn't interested in them."

"Why not?"

"Most of them went on and on about how hard it must be to be a single father. I didn't want their pity, and I am pretty capable of taking care of my kids."

"You are a good father, Brad." She sighed. "I guess we have something in common. Rick cheated on me too."

I stared at her profile as she chewed a breadstick. "I'm sorry."

"Water under the bridge now." She furrowed her brow for a moment. "My youngest, Emmy, has ASD, Autism Spectrum Disorder. It's not that she has autism. She's more in line with an Asperger's diagnosis. She can communicate pretty well, and she's intelligent, but she's socially awkward, and she's very particular—like OCD on steroids particular. Hence the reason for the call tonight. My mother did something that put her into a tantrum."

"How long ago was she diagnosed?"

"Almost three years ago. Teachers started noticing a pattern of behavior and her tendency to close herself off from others socially. She needed a strict routine, and she wasn't getting it, which caused issues. Rick didn't know how to deal with that."

"I'm sure it was hard, but that doesn't give him an excuse for straying on your marriage."

She laughed slightly. "It wasn't just that. Lauren, my oldest, was diagnosed with rheumatic heart disease two years ago. We were finally getting Emmy under control, and then Lauren was playing soccer and passed out."

"I don't know anything about that."

"I didn't either, but Lauren used to get strep throat a lot—like all the time. Sometimes it didn't seem bad, or that she even had it, but once she got it, it caused rheumatic fever, and that damaged her heart."

I reached for her hand. "I'm so sorry, Nolan. That has got to be difficult. Is there a way to cure her?"

"Not right now. We have to make sure her blood pressure stays normal, and Lauren undergoes routine tests to make sure her heart valves are working properly. Eventually, she might need a heart transplant, but we aren't there yet."

"That has to be scary for you."

"It is, but it's scary and stressful for her. She's twelve. She wants to be a normal kid. She'd love nothing more than to play sports and run around with her friends, but she can't. Sometimes I think she feels like she let me down because she can't play soccer anymore, and she knows I love to coach it."

"But you don't feel like she let you down, do you?"

"No, not at all." She stirred the pasta on her plate and then lifted her gaze to mine. "That's why I said what I did back there on the phone about not getting involved with someone. I don't have the time or energy to put into a relationship with someone else when I have all that to deal with. My kids are work, and I can't ask another man to take that on."

"Don't you think the right man would want to take that on?"

She shrugged. "I don't know. Their father doesn't want to deal with it. Would you want to take on two children that weren't yours and deal with their medical issues?"

"It depends on how I felt about their mother. I would never throw away a good thing just because two children needed medical attention."

"But it's not just medical attention, Brad. Emmy needs a lot of structure in her life. It's the main reason why I didn't bring her with me while I did this. She would not be able to deal with all the construction and change going on."

"Then it's a good thing that she is safe where she is so you can get it right for her."

"She is, but god, do I miss my girls."

"I bet you do. I can't imagine not having my children around me all the time."

"Yeah, that is something that pisses me off about Rick. He walked away and moved hundreds of miles away from the girls. He does a video chat with them once a week, if that. It's like he just turned his back on their problems and didn't want to have anything to do with them. Could you imagine doing that to your children?"

"Never, and I wouldn't do that to someone else's child either. Marisol is a good example. She's not blood to us, but she's my niece, and I'd do anything for her. If we learned tomorrow that she had a health problem, we'd all rally around her, not walk away and build a wall to protect her. That's not how my family is."

"I know. I love your family," she said almost wistfully.

"They are pretty awesome, aren't they?" I tapped my fork for a moment on my plate. "And just so you know, they are aware that we slept together."

Her eyes went wide as her fork halted an inch from her open mouth. "Why?"

I laughed. "Um, funny story," I said, and then I proceeded to tell her about it.

She threw her head back and laughed. "I can't believe you said that at the dinner table, and with your daughter there! What did she do?"

"She gave me the stink eye and left. I spoke with her later, and she understands."

"I bet she thinks a lot of me."

"I don't know what she thinks. She asked if you were going to be her new mom now." She went stone cold. "Don't worry, I told her we weren't anywhere near that."

"Well, I'm glad you said that because I was serious in what I said earlier, Brad. I'm not in a place to get involved with someone."

"Is that why you haven't been very chatty this last week?"

"Partially, and also because I was busy. I don't want you to get the wrong idea here. I like you, probably more than I should, but I can't give you that happy family that you want. I have two girls that need my attention when they move here, and I can't step into another woman's shoes for your kids at the same time."

"I'm not asking you to." I set my fork down and took her hand. "I'm only asking for your friendship and for us to get to know one another more. If something develops later, we'll deal with it then. I want to get to know you more, Nolan, and I want to help you get that house together as quickly as you can so that you can bring your girls home."

"Think we might be able to still have sex once in a while?" she asked as a small smile slipped over her lips.

I squeezed her hand and replied huskily, "Why do you think I suggested you come over here so I can give you a massage?"

# CHAPTER SEVENTEEN

## NOLAN

*I* was well aware that the only reason I told him all that was because I was tired, and my filter had expired for the day. Usually, I didn't air my dirty laundry because people would turn their noses up and talk behind my back. I knew Brad was different, though. I also knew that he liked me and that he wouldn't go around discussing my children or me.

Brad felt safe to me. He also hadn't batted an eye when I told him about the medical conditions that my children had. Some men would have run from that alone or wouldn't have even wanted to know in the first place because they were only after one thing. Brad wasn't.

Although he was alluding to sex now, and I was all for that. Forget dinner. Food could be eaten anytime. I only had a limited amount of time to enjoy the fruits of the flesh without children present. It was time to take advantage of that.

I glanced at his plate. "You done eating yet?"

He eyed my plate and then his. "How about you finish what's on your plate, and I finish mine. We drink the rest of our wine, and then I give you a massage. Does that work?"

"Would it be weird if I asked to take a shower first?"

"Not at all."

"Then it's a deal." I went back to eating with more interest than I previously had, and I noticed he was eating a bit faster, too, although we did share some general chitchat about the job he was working on now while we finished.

Once done, he put the plates in the sink and the remainder of the food in the fridge, filled our wineglasses again, and then took me by the hand and led me up the stairs.

Unlike downstairs, there were no pictures of Cheryl in the bedroom. In fact, there was nothing to remark that a woman had ever lived there. It was decorated in masculine tones, with limited items lying on the dressers. I was happy to see that because having the ghost of another woman around you could be somewhat overwhelming at times.

Rick's only presence was in the girls' rooms by way of a photograph. Anything left behind after our divorce was tossed in the trash.

Brad led me to the bathroom. "It shouldn't be too messy in there. The housekeeper cleaned two days ago."

"You have a housekeeper?"

"Yeah, I like to fix things, not clean." He chuckled.

"I might have to get her number," I told him.

"Go on in and take a shower. There are clean towels in the linen closet."

"Alright, thank you, Brad."

He paused in front of me. "You're welcome, Nolan."

I went up on tiptoe, and he leaned forward to accept the kiss I was offering. He stepped aside, and I slipped into his bathroom. I had a feeling that Milton had a hand in the design because it was gorgeous. I sure hoped that he did as well with mine.

I undressed and found a towel, and then I turned on the

water and stepped into the doorless shower. It was rather sexy. Maybe I should think of something like this for myself.

I rinsed off and then decided to wash my hair. I was surprised by Brad's shampoo choice, as it was something a woman would probably choose over a man, but I was glad he had it. After finishing, I dried myself off and wrapped the towel around my body.

When I opened the door, I was surprised to find a few candles on the nightstands and soft piano music playing from a device on the other side of the room. The lights were off, and Brad was lying on the bed in black boxer briefs. Well, hello!

"Rather romantic, Mr. Young. I like it."

"Well, we can't have bright lights and loud music while you are getting a massage to relax. Now can we?"

"No, that wouldn't go over very well."

"Kind of defeats the purpose." He patted the bed. "Come lie down, Nolan."

He didn't have to ask twice. As I dropped the towel at the side of the bed, I noticed a bottle of massage oil on the nightstand. The man had thought of everything.

I raised a brow as I climbed on the bed. "You even have massage oil."

He smirked as he checked me out. "Yeah, a gift from Riley. She was trying to talk me into getting back out there and said having that around might entice a woman to my bed. Is it working?"

I leaned forward and kissed him. "Oh, it's working alright."

He wrapped a hand around my neck and brought my lips back to his for a kiss filled with promise. I sure hoped that his massage didn't suck. That would have killed the moment.

"Lay down and get comfy," he said as he shifted off the bed.

I moved to the center of the bed and lay down, pulling one of his pillows under my cheek. I inhaled and found myself doing it a second time as his scent filled my lungs.

He climbed back on the bed, and I heard the lid of the oil snap open. "Did you enjoy your shower?"

"I did, thank you."

"Good." He drizzled a little of the oil over my back, and I hissed. He chuckled huskily. "Sorry, I should have warmed that up first."

The bottle clicked again, and then I felt it bounce on the mattress beside me. A moment later, Brad's large callous-rough hands brushed over my skin. Within a few seconds, I knew this man had more talent in his hands than for just swinging a hammer.

I sighed as I burrowed further into his pillow. He worked slowly, from the middle of my back up to my shoulders. "Do you mind if I straddle your legs?"

"I don't mind anything that you want to do," I murmured as I was lulled into comfort by the atmosphere and the wine in my system.

He chuckled softly. "That leaves me with a lot of ideas."

"Bring them on," I said sassily.

The bed shifted again as if he had gotten off, but I didn't bother to open my eyes. I was too comfortable where I was. A moment later, he was back, and he climbed over my thighs.

I enjoyed the feel of his legs against my hips as he leaned forward and a moment later felt something against my lower back. Oh, he had gotten off the bed to remove his boxers. I was all for that.

Brad continued to rub my shoulders and worked his way down my back, making sure to spend just enough time on each area and not overdo it. His hands were masterful, and I was in heaven as he continued lower. I felt his erection resting on my butt cheek as he shifted back slightly to reach my lower back. Then he moved down and began to rub each one of my cheeks, tenderly almost teasing me as his fingers moved to the area between my legs. My breath caught as he ever so slightly brushed his thumbs along my sensitive skin.

He picked up the oil, and I heard the lid open and close again before he rubbed his hands together and then began on the tops of my thighs. His hands stroked up my thighs and then down, then back up where they'd come closer to where I wanted them, but then he'd move them away again. It was an evil cat and mouse game, and I was ready for the cat to catch its prey.

After he went down to my feet, he slowly worked his way back up. When he got to my butt, he worked each cheek more carefully and then slid his hand between my legs. I was so ready for him now that I whimpered as he shifted his weight higher and began to work on my back again. As he readjusted his body, he intentionally rubbed his erection against the crack of my cheeks, and I arched toward him.

He leaned forward, kissing my shoulder and then moving my hair to kiss my neck. He ground his pelvis against me, and I arched again to add more pressure. He sat back up, shifting down my legs more so he could go back to rubbing my lower back, hips, and then he focused on the area between my thighs.

"Jesus," he murmured as his fingers ran along my slick length. He continued to rub me, and then he inserted a finger. I pushed against him, ready for more, needing more.

I moved my hands from under the pillow to down alongside myself, so that I could touch his thighs. My fingernails trailed lightly over his skin as he inserted a second finger. I glanced over my shoulder as far as I could to see him staring down between my legs, and I arched more into his hand.

He looked at me, and I bit my bottom lip as he pressed deep into me. I couldn't hold back the whimper that time. I needed more.

His ragged breathing now filled the air, and a moment later, he removed his hand and brushed his shaft against my aching flesh. He hissed as he did it a second time, and then he pressed himself slowly into me. I closed my eyes, enjoying every delicious inch of him.

I realized after a moment that he wasn't wearing a condom this time. I was glad because I could feel him better, and I knew he could feel me more as he moaned softly and pulled out to go back in.

I let him control the speed for a few moments, but then I needed more. I shifted my hips and wiggled a bit, and he withdrew. I went to my knees, and he moaned louder as I gave him my backside. He readjusted himself so that he was right behind me and pushed right back in, holding my hips tightly as he seated himself deep within me. Now that's what I needed.

I reached between my legs and rubbed the sensitive nub as he began to move. It didn't take us long to climb that precious mountain, and I was right there with him when he let himself go.

Our movements slowed, and I felt him sag slightly against me for a few seconds before he moved away and fell to the mattress. I curled on my side and smiled at him. "That was the best massage I have ever gotten."

He laughed. "You enjoyed that, huh?"

"Oh, I did." I sat up. "But I don't think we're done yet."

"We aren't?"

"No, lie back." I didn't give him much of a chance to get settled before I was climbing over his hips and fitting him back inside of me. "I'm kind of a two-orgasm girl."

"Whatever you need," he said as I began to move. For as long as I'd been having sex, I needed to have two before I was satisfied. I moved over him, and his hands brushed over my body, squeezing my breasts as he pushed up his hips. His eyes closed for a moment, and I knew that he might be forty, but the man had a lot of repressed sexuality that needed to come out. Some men at forty would have been done for a few hours, but not Brad. Nope, he was right there with me.

I rode him until I began to feel the build again, and he pushed harder, faster as I ground myself against him. I let my head fall back on my shoulders, and it slammed into me again, and a moment later, his body stiffened under me as he joined me.

I collapsed onto his chest and let my heart rate slow. "Okay, I think I'm good now."

His body vibrated with a silent laugh. "Is it weird that I totally love that you need to do that twice?"

I lifted my head and stared at him. "It only benefits you."

"True, but maybe next time we should go for three for you."

I lifted a brow. "You think you are up to that?"

He laughed. "I didn't say three for me. I was thinking more of three for you."

"Well, I'm willing to try if you are." I couldn't hold back the yawn that slammed over me.

"Why don't you go clean up, and then you can get some sleep."

"I'm not sure I can move," I replied.

"Alright, then move over and let me go." I rolled like a rag doll off of him and to the side of the bed. He went into the bathroom, and a few moments later, he returned with a wet washcloth and stared down at me. "Turn toward me."

"You're going to clean me now?" I asked with a laugh.

"Hey, I made the mess. I might as well clean it, too."

I snickered as I rolled my hips toward him. Maybe it was weird to do that with a man that I barely knew, but I wasn't modest, and he seemed all too happy to be of service.

In fact, once he was done, he climbed back on the bed and gave me a sexy as hell grin before he leaned forward, hovering over the juncture of my legs, and said, "I think we need to see if we can get the third one right now. What do you say?"

I didn't reply. I just spread my legs wider and watched Brad drop between my thighs. My god, I might kinda love this man.

# CHAPTER EIGHTEEN

## BRADLEY

*I* lay on my side and watched her sleep. Her face was toward me, and her small hand was curled under her chin. She looked almost like a child as she breathed in slowly and then released it, and my heart thudded a little harder in my chest.

I could easily fall in love with this woman. Hell, I was probably already halfway there.

She was so intense most of the time, but tonight. Tonight I had seen the fragile interior of the woman who wanted to be loved and needed help—not help with fixing her house or providing for her, but in being there for her. She needed someone to support her emotionally and love her unconditionally. Someone who wouldn't leave when the going got tough.

I lay back and stared at the ceiling. With that, Nolan also needed someone who could deal with her children. Well, not deal with them, but be able to help with them and emotionally support them also. Could I do something like that? What kind of stress would that put on my children? Would that cause issues with them to allow two more kids into their lives, ones with serious medical problems?

That was something to consider seriously as we got to know one another. I wished her girls were here and I could meet them. Then we could introduce them to my kids and see how they got along.

Would Nolan be alright with that? Or would she fight it right from the suggestion? I didn't know her well enough to know the answer to that question. I turned to look at her again. I sure wanted to know her, though, and as I drifted off to sleep, I made the plan to help her and support her the most that I could.

I woke in the morning and felt something shift beside me. Alright, it wasn't a something as much as a someone. I blinked a few times as I turned my head to find Nolan sitting upright, wearing my t-shirt, cross-legged, staring at me as she ate a yogurt.

I chuckled. "Got hungry, huh?"

She grinned as she pulled the spoon from her mouth. "Yes, not enough to eat last night and worked off quite a few calories. Hope you don't mind."

"Not at all." I pondered that for a moment and realized that it didn't bother me. I liked that she made herself at home. I rolled to my side, propping my head upon my palm. "Did you sleep alright?"

She nodded and replied thoughtfully, "I did. Even your snoring didn't bother me."

I laughed. "I don't snore."

She grinned. "I beg to differ. Maybe it's weird, but I kind of liked it."

"Yeah, how could anyone like someone else snoring?"

She hesitated, peering at me for a second before she replied, "Because it meant you were there, and I wasn't alone."

I could reply to that comment in two ways, one serious and one not so much. I choose to make light of it. "Yeah, kind of sucks sleeping alone all the time, doesn't it?"

Nolan grinned. Right answer. "It does." She scraped the spoon inside the cup for a moment. "Rick used to snore, and sometimes it got on my nerves, mostly toward the end, but in the beginning, I used to be thankful for it."

I chuckled. "Does that mean you are going to get tired of hearing me snore eventually?"

"No." She giggled. "That would require us to sleep together a lot more often, and you know that's not going to happen."

I opened my mouth to argue, but I decided against it at the last moment as she watched me carefully. "I guess we will just have to have sex during the day, so there is no sleeping involved."

She grinned. "I like that idea, and as much as I'd like to do that again right now, I need to get back to my house. I have walls to paint and a bunch of other things to get done, and Pete is coming today to work."

"Oh, yeah, that's right. Okay, well, let me get dressed, and we can head over so we can get to work." I threw back the covers and got out, trying not to be embarrassed by the morning wood I was sporting. If I thought she wasn't going to notice, I was wrong.

"Keep looking at me like that, and we aren't getting to your place anytime soon."

"Gah! Ruin a girl's fun," she commented as she climbed off the bed, but I knew she wasn't upset with me.

As she walked past me to the bathroom, I stared at her unabashedly, and I swear she put a little more swing in her step.

"You're playing with fire, young lady."

"That's cuz I like it hot," she said saucily over her shoulder before she disappeared into the bathroom. Yep, I was falling for her big-time.

After we were dressed, we headed to her place and stopped to grab breakfast at Coral's Coffee Café on the way. I offered to go in alone, but Nolan hopped out of the truck to come with me. I guessed she didn't care about people seeing her with me this early in the morning.

It was just after seven, and since it was Saturday, it wasn't that busy. Coral was behind the counter and grinned widely at me before she glanced at Nolan. I wasn't sure if Nolan saw Coral's eyebrow pop or not, but I did.

"Morning, Coral, how is your father?" Coral Winston and her family were very close to ours. We'd grown up with their very similar family. We had four boys and two girls, and they had the opposite. Coral's mother had passed away, and it had hit all of us very hard.

One of the boys in the family, Ethan, was married to my sister, Riley. They had tied the knot last year in a civil service and now had a toddler, Corey.

"He's doing okay. You know him. He just keeps going."

I smiled. "He is a strong man," I agreed with her. "Coral, I'm not sure if you have met Nolan Nickels, but she bought the old Millstone property."

"I heard there was a buyer! I've seen you in here a few times but never got the chance to introduce myself. What on God's green earth possessed you to buy that property? I hope your husband is handy." They shook hands over the counter.

"It's great to meet you, Coral," Nolan said, and before she could reply further, I jumped in.

"Actually, Nolan is doing a lot of the work herself. She even does a better job than Kayley, but don't tell my sister I said that."

We all laughed, and then Nolan spoke. "I'm actually divorced and moving here for a new start. I wanted a place that I could make my own."

Coral whistled. "Girl, I gotta give you some credit there. I don't know how a hammer even works."

"That's not true," I replied with a chuckle. "Coral did her fair share of summers helping Kayley and me when we were teens."

Coral eyed me carefully. "And you know that I only did that because I had a huge crush on you."

Nolan laughed loudly, and I glanced at her. For a moment, time stopped, and I fell just a little further.

Coral brought me back to earth. "Brad, are you helping Nolan?"

"I am. We are on our way over there now. Hence the reason we stopped in."

"Well, what can I get for you?"

After we ordered, we stepped to the side to let another customer get to the counter, and I explained to Nolan that Coral was about the same age as Henley and Riley, but she had always hung out with the older kids when we were together. I also explained that Ethan was her slightly older brother.

"Ah, that makes sense. Now that you tell me that, Coral is part of the family you grew up with, right?"

"Yeah, she is."

"Kayley told me many stories of you all. Her mother passed away not too long ago, correct?"

"Yeah." I frowned as I ran a hand over my beard. "Man, it's been almost two years already. It was in July when Riley was pregnant."

"I can't imagine losing my mother. I mean, I know that one day I will, and sometimes she just irks me something fierce, but I can't imagine not being able to pick up the phone and call her when I need her for something, or just to listen."

"Yeah, me either."

Our food was ready a few minutes later, and after we got back to the truck, she sipped her coffee, and said, "Do you think Coral knows we slept together?"

I laughed. "Why would you even ask that?"

"Because it's like seven in the morning, and both of us look a little rumpled, no offense, but we do, and we are together in one car."

"For all she knows, I picked you up at Kayley's."

"Which is on the other side of town near my house."

I glanced at the front door of the café. "Yeah, she totally thinks we slept together."

Nolan started to laugh. "That doesn't bother you, does it?"

"Me? No. What about you?"

"Nope, not at all. Let everyone see the new girl in town with the hottie construction worker." She grinned at me over her to-go cup.

"You're a trip. You know that?"

"Yep! Now let's get to my place and eat, and then I have a lot of work for you to do."

"You do, huh?"

"Yep." She glanced at her phone. "If we eat quickly, then we can try out my sleeping bag before Pete arrives at eight-thirty."

My jaw kind of dropped slightly, but instead of replying, I put the truck in reverse and pulled out of the spot as she giggled beside me.

And I just fell a little more.

W e did try out her sleeping bag, and if I weren't so damn old, I might have enjoyed it better. Both of us were of like minds when we said a mattress was better.

We were getting the walls ready in her room when Pete arrived, and for a little while, he talked over what he was going to tackle today, the first thing being the new panel.

"I guess it's a good thing that I forgot to plug in my minifridge and put stuff inside. I forgot the electricity was going to be off for a while."

"What I am going to focus on first is the panel, then the kitchen. I'll slowly branch off to the other parts of the house. I have a buddy coming at ten to help me. He will start in the kitchen while I finish up the panel. There won't be any power in most of the house for about three days. Some of upstairs will take about a week."

"It's a good thing I don't need you on-site until next Monday. You can hopefully finish this before I need you to start wiring the new house."

"That's the plan," he stated. We spoke for a few more minutes, and then we let him get started.

"Well, you ready to tackle the master?"

"I'm more than ready," she replied as we headed up the stairs. I followed behind, watching the way her hips swayed back and forth. Images of massaging those cheeks returned to me, and I had to start reciting construction terms to get my mind out of the gutter.

We were three hours into our work when I heard my son's voice downstairs. "How about we take a break. I think my mom is here with lunch."

"You know your mom doesn't need to keep doing that."

I laughed. "Yeah, you tell her that. She brings lunch to me at my worksites sometimes to make sure I eat properly."

"She's a good mom," she said as she approached me.

"She is."

Nolan put her arms around my neck and lifted on her toes to kiss me. I forgot that other people were in the house for a few moments, but fast-approaching footsteps alerted us, and we broke apart just before Tyler rushed into the room.

"I didn't know where you were," he stated.

"I'm right here. Where is the fire?"

"There isn't a fire. I was just trying to find you. Grandma brought lunch."

"I figured she did. We are coming down."

When we got downstairs, my mother looked at us sheepishly. "Tyler didn't interrupt anything, did he? I tried to stop him from rushing up the steps."

I heard Nolan laugh and turn away embarrassedly. "No, Mom. We were painting."

Off to the side, Tonya observed us, and I wondered what she thought as she studied Nolan.

# CHAPTER NINETEEN

## NOLAN

*W*hile I knew that there was no future with Brad and me, I decided to enjoy what we had as long as possible. That was the decision that I'd made this morning as I sat beside him eating a yogurt cup that I had confiscated from his fridge.

When I had woken up, I had studied him for a few moments. He was the kind of man I wished I could fall in love with and build a new life beside. Only I had two children that needed a lot of attention, and he had two children that didn't. I mean, they did, but not the type that mine did. Plus, his kids had already lost one parent, and I couldn't imagine them trying to adapt to a new woman who had children—and high-maintenance children to boot.

But until I brought the children down here, I could enjoy myself. I could enjoy Brad. I was pretty sure he understood my need to break things off once the kids got here, and I knew without a doubt that we'd remain friends.

During our fantastic lunch—thanks to his mother, Patricia—we sat on the back porch and talked while we enjoyed the spring sunshine and warm temps. Tyler was digging in my overgrown garden for worms, and Tonya watched my every move. She'd been doing that since she arrived—not just here, but in class too. All week, Tonya had been quiet in class and studied me. I had tried to pull her into conversation a few times, but she remained aloof.

Man, she was so much like Lauren. I hoped that when my kids moved down, they might be able to be friends. Maybe that would make the adjustment here a bit easier.

I went out to my car while everyone talked and dug around in the back seat for my favorite soccer ball. As I came around the corner, I called out to Tonya.

"Come out here and show me what you can do, Tonya."

"Um, no, thanks," Tonya said, looking uncomfortable.

"It's okay, Tonya. I told you I'd help you. Let's just kick it back and forth a little bit, and I'll show you a thing or two."

Patricia turned to her granddaughter. "Go on, Tonya. You were just talking about this last night."

She looked uncomfortable, but she got to her feet and came out to the grass slowly. Brad was watching her looking slightly nervous himself, but he kept his mouth shut—good man.

"Okay, I'm just going to kick it lightly to you. You trap it and then kick it back."

"Trap it? I don't know what that is."

I smiled at her and lightly tapped the ball to her. "Alright, then you kick it to me, and I'll show you how to trap it."

She kicked it, but it went wide, and I darted to the side and stopped it by putting my foot on top of it. "I trapped it. All you do is put your foot down on top of it to halt the movement. Think you can try that?"

She nodded, and I kicked it to her lightly again. She was able to stop it properly, and then I told her to kick it to me. Again, it went wide, and she groaned. "See, I suck!"

"No, you don't. You just don't know how to kick properly. Let me show you."

I dribbled the ball over to her using both my feet to keep it close to me, and then I trapped it and stepped back so that we were side by side. "When you kick and you want it to travel a distance, you don't use the toe of your foot. If you use the toe, then it's going to either go up in the air, or it's going to go wild as yours did. Kicking with your toe is usually the last resort." I squatted down in front of her and put my hand on her foot. "The inside part of your foot is what you want to use. Sometimes the outside if you are passing it, but that's a trickier move. When you go to kick, you are swinging your hip out and then bringing it back in."

I stood and showed her how you pull your leg back and bring it toward the ball a few times. "Does that make sense?"

"Yeah, I guess."

"Okay, then let's try it." I ran back out about fifteen feet away. "Go ahead. Just remember to bring your leg out and focus on the inside of your foot, making contact with the ball so that it will come to me. That's how you control the direction."

She nodded and then pulled her leg back and kicked. It was a lot closer to me this time, still off, but much better. I trapped the ball and sent it back to her. She tried it again and then again. By the time she had done it half a dozen times, she was getting the hang of it and even had a smile on her face.

"Great job!"

"Can I try?" Tyler asked as he stood off to the side and watched.

"Sure, move back, and we can make it a triangle."

We shifted our grouping a little, and then I kicked it to Tyler. He trapped it and sent it on to Tonya, who had to race a bit to the side to catch it. For a few minutes, the three of us passed the ball around, and then I popped one into the air with my toe toward Tyler, who tried to catch it.

"No hands, Tyler. You have to use your body."

He looked at me like I'd lost my mind. "How do you catch a ball with your body?"

"You don't catch it; you block it from going past you so you can take control of it and move it in the direction that you want. Throw it in the air to me."

He did, and I used my torso to stop the movement and then dribbled it toward him, spun around his body, and kicked it toward Tonya.

"Wow, she's terrific," I heard Patricia say, and Tonya and Tyler were laughing.

"Okay, guys, I need to get back to work, but you guys can keep practicing if you want. Tyler, there is another ball in the back seat of my car. You guys can practice dribbling it."

"Isn't dribbling basketball?" Tyler asked with a funny look on his face.

"Yep, it is, but it's also for soccer." I took the ball, dribbled it out about twenty feet, turned it around, and then brought it back. "You do that to take it down the field and stay in control of it until a team member is open to set up a shot for the goal. That is a drill that all soccer players do for hours and hours up and down the field."

Tyler raced off to get the other soccer ball, and then I stood on the back porch as the two of them tried their hand at dribbling. "Don't go so fast until you get used to it, and don't kick it that hard. You want to tap it lightly a few feet in front of you to keep it under control. Once you get the hang of it, then try to go a little faster."

"Okay!" Tonya yelled, and I picked up my water bottle and took a long drink.

I turned to Brad. "You ready to get back to work?"

"Yep, I am." He got to his feet, and Patricia said she would sit out back and watch the kids for a little while.

Inside, Brad followed me up the stairs, and we were barely in the bedroom before he spun me around and wrapped his arms around my waist. "Do you know how damn sexy you are?"

I laughed. "You think so, huh?"

"Yeah, I do. I loved watching you out there, and Tonya was listening to you. I was worried when she went out there because I've seen her try to play before."

"She just needs some one-on-one instruction, and she'll get it."

"Thank you," he said softly as he stared down at me.

"You're welcome. Now, are you going to kiss me so we can get back to work, or are we going to dance now?"

He chuckled and cupped my cheek. "I'll take the kiss now and the dance later."

Oh, so he liked to dance, too? Nice. "I'll hold you to that," I told him before I brushed my lips against his.

We managed to get the second coat on the walls when Patricia found us cleaning up. "This looks wonderful," she commented as she looked around.

"Thank you." I loved the light-lavender color on the walls and couldn't wait to have my furniture delivered by the movers who were waiting for me to pick a date.

She stepped into the bathroom and laughed. "Your bathroom could use a little work."

"Milton is going to do that for me. I have to pick out my tile. I forgot to do that." I went to get the tile samples and brought them back into the bathroom. "What do you think of these?" I asked her.

We discussed the tiles a little, and I found that we had similar tastes in designs. Patricia helped me decide, and I set the three tiles aside to show Milton.

"Now that I have those, I can have him get started."

"That's great. The grays will look very pretty, especially if you add in some of that lavender color from the bedroom."

"I was thinking of doing that."

She smiled kindly at me. "Thank you for helping Tonya. She was very excited that you had offered to do it."

"It's my pleasure."

"Do your kids play soccer?"

"Um, no. Lauren, my oldest, did, but she has a medical condition that doesn't allow her to play anymore right now."

"Oh, dear, I hope it's not too serious."

"We hope so too," I replied, not wanting to get too deeply into it. I was pretty sure that she'd ask Brad about it later, and he could tell her what he wanted to.

Patricia turned to Brad. "Do you need me to take them this afternoon, or are you going to be able to?"

Brad winced, and I quickly jumped in. "Go take care of your kids. You have been doing so much for me. You should spend time with them."

"You sure?"

"Yep, I am going to start working on colors for the other rooms and replace a couple of light fixtures that I got while the power is off."

"Alright, then I'll help you get this cleaned up."

"No, I got it."

Patricia said her goodbyes and said she'd see me soon, and then Brad turned back to me after he thanked his mom.

"I could drop them off at this party and come back for a little while."

"Don't you have other things that need your attention?"

He laughed. "Maybe I don't want to do those other things."

"Well, go do them. You have done so much for me."

"It has been my pleasure." He approached me and pulled me into his arms. "I happen to like working with you."

I wrapped my arms around his neck. "I think you like it better when we aren't working."

"You caught me." He grinned and then kissed me soundly. "If you need anything, just give me a shout."

"I think I'll be alright but thank you."

He stepped back slowly. "Okay, but the offer stands. Would you be interested in coming over to my parents' for dinner tonight?"

"Thank you, but no. I have things that I need to do for school."

"Okay, then I'll talk to you later. I assume you are going to be working after school here this week."

"I will, but you won't be. Spend time with your kids," I urged him nicely. It wasn't that I didn't want his help or for him to be here; I just didn't want him to get too attached.

He laughed. "I feel like I'm getting the brush-off."

Whoops! "No, not at all. I just think you should focus on your kids while you have them." I took his face in my hands. "I promise I will ask for your help when I need it. I really do appreciate everything that you have done for me. I took this project on because I wanted to do it. So far, I've had everyone else doing it. It's time for me to focus on my house alone."

"Alright, I get that, and you're welcome."

"Now, get out of here." I leaned up on my toes and kissed him one more time. As he walked out of the room, I sighed to myself.

I liked Brad more and more each time we were together, but I knew that I couldn't ask him to be part of my family. I had to keep space between us so that I didn't fall in love with him. That was the last thing that either of us needed.

# CHAPTER TWENTY

## BRADLEY

$\mathcal{U}$nlike last week, Nolan stayed in touch more over the next few days. We texted a couple of times each day and even spent thirty minutes on the phone Monday night. Since she didn't have full power in her house yet, she didn't hang around in the evenings to work late at her place.

Tuesday evening, she had soccer games and then papers to grade, and Wednesday, she went back to Summersville to get more paint and supplies.

Today was Friday, and Pete said he'd have the house back online and completed after a couple of tweaks. Sadly, they had to pull the walls apart in a few places and found a couple of problems that delayed the wiring two days, but it was done right. Nolan was working to patch those back up this weekend and start more painting.

My house build was moving along quickly, and I was working hard so that I wouldn't have to do more hours on the weekend. I'd much rather spend them helping Nolan than another customer. Although my customer was paying me, and she wasn't.

I hoped that Nolan would be receptive to coming over to my place tonight. Right after work, I was taking the kids out to Summersville to stay with Wes and Charlotte. They were taking the kids to the lake on tomorrow for a work picnic that Wes had for the hospital.

I was also hoping for a few minutes to speak with Wes alone when I dropped them off. Luckily, the opportunity presented itself as he handed me a beer, and we went to sit on his back deck.

"How are things going?" he asked after taking a sip of his drink.

"Busy, but good." I proceeded to tell him about the house I was working on, and he listened patiently and then stared at me hard. "What?"

"I was more wondering how things with Nolan were going. I was pretty sure you had your job under control."

I laughed. "Better *and* worse than I expected."

"Better and worse? How is that?"

I hesitated for a moment, then sighed. "I like her."

"Is that the better or worse part?"

I laughed. "The better part."

"And the worst part is she doesn't like you back?"

"No, I think she does." I took a drink. "The problem is that she has said several times that once she has her kids back, that things with us need to cool down."

"Cool down? Or stop?"

"Stop."

"Why would she say that?"

"Because both of her kids have medical conditions, and I think she's concerned that I won't be able to deal with them or that it would cause problems with my kids."

He studied me carefully. "Are those her worries, or yours?"

"Maybe both," I told him with a slight shrug.

"What medical conditions do they have?"

"Her older daughter has a heart condition caused by an infection."

"She probably has rheumatic heart disease. That is a tough one."

"Yeah, that sounds like what she told me. The younger one is on the autism spectrum. She told me a little about it, but I don't know anything about that stuff, so it doesn't exactly make sense to me."

Wes inhaled deeply and then released it. "Both could be tough to deal with, but if you are wondering if you could do it, I know you could. You are a very patient man, Brad. More patient than any of us. If anyone could learn to deal with those types of things, it's you."

"But what would it do to Tonya and Tyler?"

He shrugged. "I don't know. I think they would have a harder time adjusting to the fact that you share your life with three other people now. They have had you alone for a long time. I'm sure Tyler doesn't even remember Cheryl."

"He doesn't."

"I think he would adjust better than Tonya." He eyed me. "What did she have to say about your blurted announcement last week?"

I chuckled. "We discussed it, and I explained that I liked Nolan and that sex as an adult is different than sex as a young person."

He smirked at me. "Is it?"

"Well, no. I guess not. Damn, Wes. I like Nolan. I could see myself falling in love with her and building a life."

"Do you think she feels the same?"

"I don't know. I know Nolan likes me, but because she keeps saying that we can't have a future, I'm not sure if she's even considered it. As far as I know, she thinks what we are having is an affair, and she is going to walk away from it as soon as her kids get here."

"Then if you want more, you need to tell her. I'd also research what her kids are dealing with and see if you think you can handle it. Starting a new relationship is tough. Blending a family is tough. Add in a blended family, a new relationship, and two kids who need medical attention, and that's a whole new level of stress."

"I guess you are right."

"I like what she's done for you."

"What do you mean?"

"I mean, you look happy. I haven't seen you look like this for a long time."

"Yeah, I guess it's been a few years since I felt this way."

"You've been down and quiet since before Cheryl even found out she had cancer."

I turned to him. "You noticed that, huh?"

He nodded. "Did you know she was having an affair?"

I blinked. "How the hell did *you* know that?"

"I saw them out together one night. I made sure she didn't see me, but she looked happy, and I knew you weren't. I tossed it back and forth whether I should say something to you, and I had finally decided to tell you what I knew, but then you told us that she had stage-four cancer. I figured there was no reason to bring it up then."

"Yeah, I knew. We had already talked about getting a divorce."

"You hung around, though, even though you knew what you were in for. That says a lot about you, Brad. You're willing to stick by someone that you care about and have made a commitment to. If you decided to take the chance on Nolan and her kids, I know you would do right by them."

"You think so?"

"I do. The hardest part would be making sure Tyler and Tonya could adjust to it."

"How do I do that?"

"First thing is they need to meet. Before the kids do, you might want to share with them what's up so that they don't ask uncomfortable questions. If they are aware of the conditions beforehand, you might help school them on how to handle things smoothly. They are either going to like them or not. You won't be able to force it."

"What if they don't? What if I realize that I love Nolan and that I want a future, and then the kids don't get along?"

"Did we get along all the time?"

I laughed. "No, we didn't, but I'm not sure what would happen with the relationship that I am trying to build with Nolan."

"That is something the two of you would have to discuss. I only met Nolan once, but she seemed pretty open to discussing things. If you told her that you wanted to make it work, then I bet you two could find a way to make that happen."

"Maybe," I said as I stared out over the yard. "I'd like it too. I really can see myself falling in love with her."

"You sure you're not already?"

I contemplated that for a moment. "Maybe I am a little bit."

"Then you need to have these conversations sooner rather than later. If you want a future with Nolan, then you need to tell her. I know you guys haven't known each other long, but there is too much at stake here not to. Ask her how she feels. Ask her if she thinks a future is possible, and tell her you're open to learning how to cope with things to make life easier for her."

"You know, I thought about that before. I want to be there for her. She's a really strong woman, and she doesn't need someone to do the heavy work, but emotionally, she's alone. I hate that."

"You were emotionally alone for a long time, Brad. You see

yourself in her, and that's why you want to be there for her. You found someone who can understand you."

"Her husband had an affair on her too. He left Nolan to be with the other woman after his daughter was diagnosed with the heart condition."

"That's low."

"I know. I keep thinking about when Cheryl found out she had cancer. The last thing I considered was walking away. I probably would have been there for her even if she had chosen the other guy."

He laughed. "You probably would have been. That's the kind of guy you are, Brad. You live up to your commitments. A lot of men run from them and trouble. The fact that you are even thinking about this and wondering if you could handle it tells me you can. You're thinking ahead and not just letting your hormones rule your body."

I snorted. "Yeah, well, when I'm around her, it's hard not to listen to those."

"A healthy sex life is good for a relationship."

"It's healthy, alright."

Wes laughed, and for a few moments, we were quiet. "If you find out more about the girls' conditions, let me know, and I'll see what information I can get you on them."

"I would appreciate that, Wes."

"Anytime, big brother. That's what family is for."

I stared at my beer. "I can't believe you knew Cheryl was having an affair."

"Henley knows too. He was out with me the night we saw her."

"Are you serious?"

"Yeah."

"If Henley knows, then Hunt knows, which means that Riley knows too. Kayley is probably the only one who doesn't."

He looked sheepish. "She knows, and so do Mom and Dad.

We discussed it one day. They were the ones that told me I needed to pass the information along to you."

My mouth hung open. "You all knew? I can't believe you all knew and never said anything."

"What was the purpose? Cheryl was dying. We all cared about her, and yeah, maybe we were a little upset about what she did, but she gave us Tonya and Tyler, and we were okay with that."

"Wow, just wow," I said as I shook my head. "I had no idea any of you knew."

"That's how we wanted it."

"Is there anything else you know that no one has told me?"

He grinned around his beer bottle. "Yeah, we all know you aren't a magnum."

I threw my head back and laughed, and for a few minutes longer, we talked. After I finished my beer, I said goodbye to the kids and hugged my brother.

"Thanks, Wes. I appreciate the talk."

"What are you going to do now?" he asked as he walked me to my truck.

"I'm going to go see Nolan and hopefully have a long talk before I get her back in my bed."

He slapped my back. "You might want to wait until after the sex part. If Nolan gets upset, you might miss out on a good time, and now that you are off the celibacy wagon, you're going to miss it."

I snickered. "Maybe you are right."

I said goodbye to him and got back on the road. I glanced at the clock and saw that it was almost seven. I grabbed something from a drive-thru on my way and then began to contemplate what I would say to Nolan tonight.

Talking to Wes had helped me make a decision. I wanted Nolan in my life, and I wanted to get to know her kids. I had visions of a blended family, and I hoped like hell that she was up for seeing that through. If not, I knew that what we had started to build needed to go on hold.

I couldn't keep seeing her, especially as my feelings were growing by leaps and bounds, if she couldn't see a future. It wasn't fair to either of us.

Man, please let there be a future.

# CHAPTER TWENTY-ONE

## NOLAN

$\mathcal{I}$t had been another long week, and I was glad it was Friday. I was ready to unwind with a glass of wine and maybe a foot rub if I could talk Brad into it. He had sent me a message a little while ago and asked if he could stop by to see me.

I knew that his kids were gone again tonight, and I had big plans for him. I thought about my sleeping bag upstairs. Tonight was supposed to be my first night in my house now that I had water and electricity, but I could pass on it one more night if I could sleep beside Brad.

I was on video chat with the girls, and Emmy was once again telling me about the new stuffed animal that she had added to her collection. She had shown it to me six times, but that's what she did. When she was happy about something, she was complexly focused on that one thing and talked incessantly about it. Sometimes it was animals, other times weather, and tonight it was her stuffed toys.

I heard the front door open and close, and I tensed. Emmy was in the middle of talking, and I couldn't cut her off, so I made a quick decision to stay on the call as Brad peeked around the corner.

I smiled at him and lifted my phone. He nodded, and instead of coming closer to me, he started looking around at the work completed this week. A few things he looked contemplative about, others he merely noticed and then moved on.

"Mom, what are you looking at?" Lauren asked as she pushed Emmy out of the way.

"Nothing," I said almost guiltily. In all honesty, I had been stalking Brad's every move.

"Yes, you are." She laughed.

Well, I might as well introduce them. Brad was a friend, and they would eventually meet him in person. "My friend just showed up."

"Kayley?"

"No, Brad. He is Kayley's older brother. He's been helping me with some things here at the house." I waved Brad over as he heard his name.

He stepped behind me. "Brad, that is Lauren on the right and Emmy on the left."

"Hey, ladies. How are you tonight?"

Emmy immediately clammed up, but Lauren was checking him out.

"Hi, we're okay. How are you?"

"Pretty good."

"What are you doing to help my mom?" she asked, and as Brad was standing slightly behind me, he rested his hand on my lower back. It made me somewhat nervous, but I knew the girls couldn't see it.

"I'm in construction and build houses. I've been helping your mom with a few things and lending her some of my employees."

I turned to Brad and laughed. "Lending? If you were lending them to me, then wouldn't the work be done for free?"

He shrugged as he grinned at me. "Not necessarily."

I almost leaned forward and kissed him but remembered that the girls were watching. "Okay, young ladies. I need to get going so we can get to work."

"Mom, it's after eight. Are you going to work tonight?"

"Yep, we have lots to do."

"It was nice to meet you girls," Brad said as he waved and then stepped away.

"Bye," both of them said, and Lauren glanced at her sister as if surprised that she had spoken. I was.

"I love you both, and I'll talk to you tomorrow."

"Have fun working," Lauren said with a smirk.

"We will. Good night, ladies. I love you."

"Love you too," they said in chorus, and then I ended the video chat.

"Sorry about that," I said as I set my phone aside. A second later, I received a text from Lauren and picked it back up. *He's cute.* I chuckled. "And Lauren thinks you're cute."

"Ha! I won half the battle. Tell her I said thank you," he replied, and I shook my head, not taking his words to heart.

I typed back the words, *he said thank you,* and she replied with an *OMG u told him! UGH!*

I laughed and slipped my phone into my back pocket as Brad approached me. "She's right. You are pretty cute."

"Yeah, well, so are you," he said huskily. "And sexy as hell in those cut-off shorts."

I turned in a circle. "You like them?"

"Yeah, I do, but I might like them better on my bedroom floor."

I fell against him. "Oh, well, that might be a possibility." I waited for the kiss that I knew was coming, and when we finished, he cupped my cheek, brushing his thumb over my skin.

"Would it be weird for me to say that I've been looking forward to tonight for the last couple of days?" Brad asked.

"Not any weirder than me thinking the same thing."

"You want to get out of here and go back to my house?"

"You have any more wine?"

"Yes."

"I know you can rub backs, but can you rub feet as well?"

"Only if you let me nibble on your toes," he said with a straight face, and I busted up laughing as I pushed him away.

"You are not allowed to chew on my toes."

He chuckled. "I didn't say chew. I said nibble. There is a difference."

"Gross! You cannot do anything to my feet besides rub them."

His sigh was exaggerated. "Fine. Take all my fun away."

I smacked his shoulder playfully. "That is not my idea of fun, but I can think of a few other things that are."

"What are we waiting for?" He waggled his brows as he took my hand and pulled me toward the door.

"Wait, I have to turn off the lights." I stopped and grinned at him. "I have to turn off the *new* electricity in my *new* house."

"Pete said the job turned out pretty well. I heard from him a little while ago."

"I hope he didn't say I was an ogre to work with."

Brad laughed heartily. "Um, no. Just the opposite. He said he wished all clients were as nice as you were."

"Aw, that was sweet of him."

It took a couple of minutes to get everything turned off because I tugged Brad around the house to show him every little thing that I had done since the last time he was here.

Finally, we were leaving to head to his house. This time I drove myself because I had soccer games to go to early in the morning.

When we arrived, we entered together, and I had barely made it over the threshold before the door closed loudly and his arms banded around me. His mouth crashed into mine, and I went with it, hopping into his arms and locking my legs around his waist as he shifted to put my back against the door that he'd just closed.

His kiss was hungry as if he had been starving for it, and it made my heart race as he held the sides of my face and deepened it even more. I was drunk on his kiss when he finally pulled back. My head bounced off the door behind me, and he chuckled softly.

"It's a good thing you and the door are holding me up because I'm not sure my legs would work right now."

"I've been dying to kiss you like that since I walked in your house tonight."

"Well..." I leaned forward and brushed my lips over his as I stroked his bearded cheek. "I've been dying for a kiss like that all week."

"I'm glad to hear that. You think your legs would hold you up now?"

"Yeah, probably."

"Would you like a glass of wine?"

"You read my mind."

"White or red?"

I shrugged. "Whatever you prefer."

"Whatever I prefer? Don't you prefer one to the other?"

"Not really." I gave him a cheesy smile. "I just love wine."

I followed him into the kitchen. "I had to go out and buy two soccer balls this week."

"You did?"

"Yeah, Tonya was complaining about not being able to practice, and Tyler said he might try out for the soccer team in middle school."

"You didn't tell him that anyone who wants to play can, did you?"

He shook his head. "No, he'll figure that out when he gets there."

"I'm glad Tonya enjoys it. I'll have to show her a few more things to help build her skills. Before you know it, she'll be right up there with the rest of the girls."

"Does it bother you or your kids that you coach soccer, and they can't play?"

I shook my head. "No, not really. Lauren was disappointed that she couldn't play, but she doesn't love it as much as I do. I asked her if she wanted me to stop, but she told me to keep doing what I love."

"Those are strong words from a young lady."

I pursed my lips as a sadness fell over me. "She grew up a whole lot when she was diagnosed. It was a scary situation for all of us, and with all the testing she went through and all the appointments she has had to attend, she's been a trooper."

"I'm not sure I could have been as strong as you have been if that had been one of my kids."

"Trust me. I had my moments when I fell apart. Mostly in the shower, but there were a few times that I crawled into the closet with a pillow over my face to hide the sobs. Plus, a time or two, I lost my shit in the car and tried to break my steering wheel as I slammed my hands on it."

He gave me an understanding smile. "I can believe that."

"But we do what we have to for our kids."

"That we do."

He grew quiet for a moment and then came around the counter, holding out a wineglass. After I took it, he captured my hand, laced his fingers with mine, and brought me to the couch. "I wanted to talk to you about something."

"Talk?" I laughed because the look in his eye said this was something serious, and I didn't want to talk seriously. I preferred to get hot and bothered. I'd even let him nibble on my toes if we could avoid talking. "I can think of more fun things to do."

"Yes, I can too, but I think we need to have this conversation." I tried not to sigh out loud. I really did. It didn't work, though. "Have a seat."

I kicked off my sandals and curled my feet under me in the corner of his sofa. He sat toward the middle of the couch and studied me for a moment before he took a long sip from his glass. I didn't want to have this conversation, so there was no way I would make it easier on him.

"I know you said that you didn't want a relationship."

"I did."

"And I know you said that what we had would end when your kids arrived."

"I did."

He paused. "What if it didn't?"

"Brad, there are reasons for why I said that."

"What reasons?"

I blew out a frustrated breath. "I can't be involved with someone right now. Not with having to deal with my kids, my job, coaching, *and* my house."

"But if you were involved with someone, they could help. *I* could help."

"You don't know what you're asking for."

"You are correct; I don't know precisely what I am asking for. What I do know is that I like you. I like you a hell of a lot more than I ever thought I would for barely knowing you. I like helping you with things, and we get along better than I have ever gotten along with any woman before. We talk, we laugh, and I'm sure that if the situation arose, we'd cry together too."

"Brad, my life is not easy. Emmy alone is not easy. I cannot bring you into my life because it's not just you. You have two kids of your own to think about. It's not like you're divorced, and your kids live full time with your estranged spouse, and we'd only have to deal with four kids every other weekend and two weeks in the summer. I will not ask you to take on the stress and frustration that I have dealt with. Not when it will affect not only you, but us as a couple and your children. I won't ask you to do that."

"I'm offering, Nolan. You aren't asking. I want to help."

Frustration exploded in me, and I uncurled my feet and put them on the floor as I set my wineglass down. "You can't help this, Brad. I don't need or want the help with this."

"Nolan, everyone needs help. I have my family to assist me, but who do you have? I want to fix that. I want to be there for you and your girls."

I ground my teeth and slowly stood. Brad came to his feet as I skimmed my angry eyes around the room. They landed on my purse before I looked at him and spoke.

"I am not a house that needs fixing, Brad. My family does not need to be fixed. You cannot *fix* my children, and I do not need a man in my life to *help* me. I can do it *myself*."

I spun and started to walk away as I fought the urge to cry. I got about two feet before a hand grabbed my arm and pulled me to a stop.

"Nolan, damn it. Don't you see how much I care for you? Don't you see that I've fallen for you?"

I pulled my arm from his grasp. "Well, then I guess it's you that needs fixing from your fall. I'm sorry, Brad, but I was honest with you at the start of all this, and I have not changed my mind."

I left him gaping at me as I grabbed my purse and hightailed it out of the house.

# CHAPTER TWENTY-TWO

## BRADLEY

*T*he front door closed, and I continued to stare at it. I blinked twice, and then I was moving. I practically ripped the door off the hinges as I yanked it open and rushed out to stop her. I didn't grab her arm this time. Instead, I jumped in front of her to block her path.

"Don't you dare tell me that you don't feel what I feel, Nolan. I know you do. I know you care about me as much as I care about you."

"Brad, move."

"Nolan." I took her face in my hands and noticed that her eyes were glassy as if she were fighting the urge to cry. Jesus, were we already going to get to that 'cry together' part? "Baby, I know you care. I know you are afraid that you will let someone into your life, and they will let you down. I am *not* that man. I will not run from a problem. I know that it could be tough blending our families, but harder things have happened. *We* could do it. I want to do it."

She blinked at me, and a tear slipped out and eased down her cheek. "You're right, Brad. I do care, but I care more about my girls than I do about you. They come first—they will always come first. What we have—what we had, was fun. It was great, and the sex was incredible, but I can't give you more. Please understand that. I have been honest with you from the beginning. I can't be what *you* want, and you are not what I need."

Not what she needed? I let my hands drop from her face as the pain of her words stabbed through my veins. "I'm not what you need? You are trying to tell me that there is another man out there that can give you more? Yeah, maybe they can give you more things, but they cannot give you their heart. Not like I can. They can't give you understanding—not as I can! They can't give you an understanding extended family, not like I can!"

"Oh, don't you dare use your family in this right now! This has nothing to do with your family, Brad. We are talking about *us*. God, Brad! Don't destroy the friendship that we built. Don't make it awkward between us. Don't make me have to *avoid* you."

I startled back slightly. "You'd do that?"

She shook her brown hair back from her beautiful face and lifted her chin. The sadness in her brown eyes was gone as resignation filled them with a fierceness that I had to admire. "If I had to, yes. I would."

"Wow!" I exclaimed as I stepped back. "I thought I knew you better, but I guess I don't know you that well after all."

"I guess you don't." She stepped around me, and this time, I let her leave. I watched her get into her car, and she glanced my way briefly before she put it in reverse and backed into the street. A moment later, she was gone.

I sighed as I shook my head, and then I went into my house and gently closed the door. Wes was right. I should have waited until after sex to have this conversation. Maybe that might have had her in a better mood.

I sank onto the sofa and stared at her wineglass. Or maybe it wouldn't have. Nolan had been honest in saying that she couldn't give me anything other than a good time. She had been brutally honest in saying that once her kids came back, it was over.

If we hadn't had this talk tonight, would that have been the case? Or would we possibly have built something strong enough to get past that?

I guess it didn't matter now since I'd never find that out.

Another week went by, and I hadn't heard a word from Nolan. I'd heard plenty *about* her, but the two of us hadn't spoken—not even one single text message.

Milton told me the master bathroom was done, and he was designing the other two now. Chester had worked on her foyer and shared that one of his buddies, Ralph, was redoing her porch. None of them asked me what had happened and why I hadn't been around to see the place or Nolan.

At the last family dinner, I learned that Cameron and Kayley had helped her install her cabinets in the kitchen, and the countertops were being delivered this next week. Kayley never said anything directly about Nolan but talked about the work as if it were a project another client had commissioned.

I also didn't ask for further details.

I was working late on the jobsite when I heard a car pull up out front. I figured it was the homeowner coming to check on the progress. They had mentioned that they might stop by.

Wes's voice rang down the hallway as I worked on the drywall in the kitchen. "I'm back here," I called out.

His footsteps echoed down the hall over the plywood floor. "Hey, it's looking pretty good. This is a nice neighborhood."

"It is a nice neighborhood. The owners got the property for a steal because the developers needed to get moving on another development—hence the reason I'm building it and not them. What brings you over this way?"

"I was dropping Marisol off at Mom and Dad's and wanted to pass something along to you."

"Yeah, what's that?"

He held a stack of papers out to me, and I took them. On the front page, it said, 'What to expect with ASD.' I lifted my eyes to him. "What's this for?"

"That is information about Nolan's kids. Kayley told me what they are dealing with, and I pulled information about it for you. I also gave you several websites you could look through and the phone numbers of a friend and specialist for each condition."

"Why would you give this to me?"

Wes looked at me like I was stupid. "You know, you once stepped in when I wouldn't listen and helped me get Charlotte back in my life. If it weren't for you getting involved, I never would have found out the truth or gotten her back." He paused. "I'm returning the favor."

"Pft, yeah, well, Nolan doesn't want me back. She's not interested in a relationship. She made it perfectly clear that she was just interested in sex with me and nothing else."

"Because she's afraid that you won't be able to handle it. Having a child on the spectrum is tough. Having another child with a coronary issue is even tougher. Both of those are scary on their own. Stack them on top of one another, and damn, man." He shook his head. "It's a recipe for stress."

"I'm aware of that. I tried to tell Nolan that too. I told her I wasn't afraid of helping, but she pushed me away."

"Brad, do you love her?" I looked away, and he touched my arm. "Do you love her?"

"Yes."

"Then don't tell her you want to help. *Show her* that you aren't afraid of helping. Learn about the conditions so that you understand them. Learn what you need to do and what you shouldn't do, then show her that you know what you're doing. Show her that you can handle it."

"How do I do that? She won't even talk to me. I'm not sure if she would speak to me if we bumped into each other on the street."

He smirked. "She'll talk to you. She's going to be at the Memorial Day picnic, *and* she's bringing her kids."

"What? How come I didn't know that?"

"Maybe because you've had your head up your ass and weren't paying attention. I don't know, but she's going to be there. I suggest that you read that information, do some more research. Call those doctors that I added to the back with any other questions, and then at the picnic, show her you're not afraid of what she fears."

I thought about that for a moment. "Do you think that would work?"

"If anything is going to work, it will be that, but if you really want this, then you need to sit down with Tonya and Tyler and talk to them about it too. Tell them that you care about Nolan and that she's afraid that they won't like her kids because they have medical conditions. Explain them to the kids so that they understand, and then when they meet her children, they can go from there."

"What if they don't understand?"

"Those two are smart kids. They spend so much time with adults that they are much more mature than their peers. I think both of them would surprise you."

"I don't know about that."

"I do." He glanced around. "This really is a nice house."

"It is."

"Did you hear that they are expanding the local hospital to include a trauma unit?"

"No, I didn't."

"Yeah, I've put in for the pediatric spot."

"Seriously?"

"Yeah, no one else knows besides Charlotte, so don't tell anyone. I don't want to get Mom and Dad's hopes up if it doesn't go through."

"Then you'll be close to home again."

"Yep, I will, and I might need someone to build me a new house."

"Oh, so that's why you are scoping this one out."

He smirked. "Yep, just a little bit. Mind if I look around?"

"Not at all."

A voice at the door called out. "That's the owner. I'll introduce you to him and show you both around."

"Hey, Myron, Elise, it's great to see you guys again. This is my brother Wesley. He stopped by to drop something off, and I was going to give him a tour. Now I can show you all, plus I have a couple of questions that we need to address."

After a brief conversation between Wes and the homeowners, we made our way around the house. I pointed out things that I had questions about, and some were answered right then. Others questions would be answered in a day or two.

Wes followed along, with their approval, and said he liked the design. It was giving him ideas for his own place.

After they all left, I finished what I had previously been doing and then decided to call it a night. Before I left, I retrieved the information that Wes had dropped off and brought it with me.

Maybe Wes was right, and I could prove to Nolan that I was up for the challenge. I'd have to read the information he gave me and do my own research. If I felt that I could handle it, I'd speak to the kids. I didn't want to get their hopes up. Tonya had already asked me why I wasn't helping Nolan anymore, and I had given her a generic response of being busy with my own work.

I had just over a week to decide if I wanted to pursue Nolan and also learn as much as I could. I would need to figure out a way to prove to her that I could handle it and not run from the hard work it would take.

After eating, showering, and watching a movie with the kids, I crawled into bed with the papers and began to read. I ended up getting my laptop and doing more research, looking up the sites that Wes had given me. It was almost midnight when I finally turned off the light.

I had learned a lot tonight, and I would continue to learn more over the next week. The one big thing that I knew was that I could handle this, and I would work with my kids to understand it so they could learn to handle it too.

I was determined to prove to Nolan that I was the right man for her and that with my kids, we could make our two broken families complete.

# CHAPTER TWENTY-THREE

## NOLAN

*I* didn't break down and cry until I was back at my house. I told myself that it was because I'd miss out on sex, but deep down inside, I knew better.

Brad had said that he had fallen for me. I couldn't admit it to him, and I didn't want to admit it to myself, but I had fallen for him too.

He was so easy to talk to, and we got along so well—in and out of bed. I loved his humor and his serious side. I loved how much his family meant to him, and honestly, I loved that he had wanted to try and take on my family.

I just couldn't let him make that sacrifice. Not with two great kids of his own. If he didn't have kids, then maybe, but what happened if we had four kids in one house and something happened between us. That would break four additional hearts, or at least three because Emmy was pretty closed off emotionally.

I sat in the corner of my kitchen and thought back on the last several weeks and every moment with him—from demoing my kitchen, to making love to him. I wiped the tears away after a while and went up to my room. I was exhausted, and I didn't have the energy to do anything more than climb into my sleeping bag. I was asleep minutes after I closed my eyes.

~

The pad that I had under my sleeping bag was not that thick, and my bones hurt every morning when I woke up. Several times I had thought about going back to Kayley's to sleep, but was determined to stay in my new home despite the uncomfortableness. One of the teachers I worked with suggested getting an air mattress, and I wasn't sure why I hadn't thought about that myself. Today, after the soccer games, I was going to head out and buy one.

I was at the soccer game, and it had just ended when Tonya sidled up to me with a smile. I glanced around but didn't see Brad with her, and I was both thankful and regretful at once.

I owed Brad an apology. He had put his heart out there, and I had whacked it with a sledgehammer. What a bitch I had been. Somewhere in our conversations, I should have told him never try to talk to me about something serious when I was close to delirium. I couldn't see around my own emotions then.

I smiled at Tonya as she stopped near me. Even though I had Tonya in my class and I'd seen her every day, we hadn't spoken about anything more than math. I had considered many times asking about her father, but decided that wasn't a good idea. Something in her eyes said he was about to come up in conversation.

"Hi, Ms. Nickels. How are you?"

"Hi, Tonya. I'm good. Did you enjoy the game?"

"I did. I've been practicing a lot."

"I'm glad to hear that. You ready to practice with the team?"

"Um, not yet, but maybe soon."

"Well, soccer is almost over for this year, but keep practicing, and next fall, you can play with the team. How does that sound?"

"Um, will you help me more?"

I wanted to tell her yes, but how could I do that when I wasn't talking to her father? After the way I had left things, I was pretty sure he wouldn't want to see me at all.

"Of course," I told her because I didn't know how to explain it. "But I am pretty busy right now. Maybe over the summer, I can help you."

"Okay." She hesitated like she wanted to say more but wasn't sure how to start.

"Is there something you want to say, Tonya?"

"Um..." Her following sentence tumbled out quickly. "Do you like my dad?"

Oh, boy. Why did I ask if there was something else? "Yes, I do like your father."

She chewed her lip nervously. "Did you break up with him?"

I averted my gaze for a moment. "Did your dad say something to you?"

She shook her head. "He's just really quiet again. For a while, he was smiling all the time, and he seemed happy, but now he doesn't."

Well, damn. "Tonya, come have a seat here for a moment."

She followed me over to the bleachers, and we sat on the bottom row. "Your dad and I weren't really dating. We were just friends, but what we want for the future isn't the same thing."

"Why not? What did you want?"

"That's kind of a complicated answer."

"I don't know. I always thought that if you liked someone, you should let them know, and if they liked you back, you would be together. That's what happened with all my aunts and uncles and in the movies I watch."

"Normally, that would be the case, but things are different with us—or maybe I should say with me."

"I don't understand."

How did I explain this to a twelve-year-old? I thought for a second. "You haven't met my children yet. I hope you meet them soon; you and Lauren are the same age."

"We are?"

"Yep."

"Cool, I can show her around the school. Maybe she can show me tips for soccer too."

"She doesn't play soccer."

She looked slightly confused. "What sport does she play?"

I sighed. "Lauren is sick. She has a bad heart, so she can't play sports anymore."

Tonya looked around, and her hands fidgeted in her lap for a minute. "What else does she like to do?"

"She likes puzzles and reading."

"I do too. We could do that together."

"That's really sweet of you, Tonya. I bet when Lauren gets here, then she would love to do that with you."

"Does your other daughter play soccer?"

I shook my head.

"Does she have a heart problem too?"

"No. Have you ever heard of autism?"

"Yeah. I have a girl in my class with it."

"You do?" I asked, surprised.

"Yeah." She grinned momentarily, then grew serious. "Does your daughter have autism?"

"Emmy has something similar to it. She's Tyler's age."

"Oh, well, does she go to normal school? Beth didn't for a while. She went to a special school, but now she goes with us, and there are five of us that help her. Each day one of us is her buddy to help her with work and projects."

"That's pretty cool."

"Yeah, she's funny. She likes to say that she's odd or strange, but we told her she isn't. She's quirky. That's what we tell her."

"Quirky? Hmm, I guess that would describe Emmy too."

"When will they move here?"

"This summer. I might bring them down Memorial Day weekend to see the house."

"You should bring them to Grandma's for the picnic."

"I might. Kayley was telling me how much fun you all have."

"Do they like horses?"

"I don't know. I don't think the girls have ever seen a horse up close."

"That's cool! They can meet Buttercup and Fellow."

"I bet they would like that."

She thought for a moment. "You said that it was complicated with my dad, but I didn't hear anything that was that hard."

I laughed softly. I was amazed at how easily Tonya had accepted what I had told her. Had I made more out of all of it than there was? Would his kids be able to accept mine?

I guess it didn't matter because I had already blown up that bridge.

"Maybe when you are older, you'll understand. I do like your father very much, but we are just friends."

She dropped her chin to her chest. "Oh, okay."

"Hey, why so sad?" She shrugged. "Tonya, what's wrong?"

She didn't look at me as she replied, "I liked him when he was happy. I was hoping he would stay like that, and—" She stopped talking.

"And what?"

"You'll think it's stupid."

"Never."

She peered at me from under her brown bangs. "I was kind of hoping you might marry him, and then I'd kind of have a mom again."

Oh, my god! I wanted to bawl my eyes out. Brad and I had barely been together, and here I was, breaking her heart already.

I put my arm around her. "Oh, Tonya, that's not stupid at all. I bet you miss having a mom."

"I do, but I don't remember too much about her."

"It's hard to lose someone when you are that young. I get it."

I lifted her chin and wiped the tear that was on her cheek. "I might not be your mom or your stepmom, I should say, but that doesn't mean I can't be your friend and love you."

"You could be? I mean, you could be my friend too?"

"Absolutely!" I hugged her tightly, and then one of the girls on my soccer team, Michelle, came running up to us.

"Tonya, we have to go. I thought you were with my parents."

"Sorry, I was talking to Ms. Nickels."

"You get going, and we will talk again soon."

"Okay," she said, and then Michelle and Tonya raced off together. I watched Tonya run, and my heart ached. I missed seeing Lauren run like that. I missed seeing Emmy period.

Maybe I *should* bring them down for Memorial Day. I could take them home the day after. They'd miss a day of school, but it was the end of the year. It wasn't like they were learning anything right now. I'd have to speak to Kayley and see if that would be alright to do.

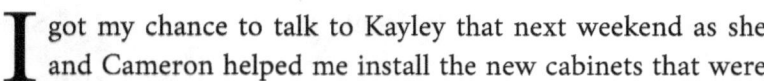

I got my chance to talk to Kayley that next weekend as she and Cameron helped me install the new cabinets that were delivered.

"Hey, Kay, I wanted to talk to you about the picnic."

She gave me a stern look. "Don't say you aren't coming because Brad is going to be there."

I had told Kayley that Brad and I had parted ways, but the only reason I gave her was that we wanted different things. She had known there was more to the story, and if she wanted to ask her brother, she could. I didn't want to cause tension in his family because I was a neurotic mess.

"No, I'm going to be there. I told you, Brad and I are friends."

"Yeah, when is the last time you spoke with him?"

I waved a hand. "That's beside the point. The reason I was bringing up the picnic is that I'd like to know if I could bring the girls."

"What? Of course! They are always invited, but I thought you weren't bringing them down until later this summer."

"I was thinking about bringing them down for the weekend and taking them back Tuesday morning."

"That would be great. I bet the girls would love to see the house too."

"We might need to crash at your place. I'm not sure if Emmy would be able to deal with the house without furniture in it, and so much still being worked on."

"Absolutely! I'll have Becky stay at my parents' house for the weekend, and you can sleep in her room. That way, the girls will have the guest room to share."

"Thank you."

"Don't thank me. You are family, which means they are family. My parents will be thrilled. I'll let them know."

I almost said, can you not tell them, but I kept my mouth shut. If Kayley told her parents, Brad would find out, and I didn't want to make him or his kids uncomfortable. "Great," I replied finally.

By the end of the day, we had most of the cabinets in place. The counters were coming on Monday, and I hadn't been able to get off work or out of coaching, so Kayley said she'd oversee the delivery. With her here, I wouldn't have to worry about it. She knew more about the installation than I did.

I stood back and looked at my kitchen. Tuesday afternoon, the appliances would be delivered, and I couldn't wait to cook my first meal in my kitchen. I had no pots or pans yet, but I was pretty excited about using my fancy new microwave.

That night as I lay on my air mattress, I wondered if I should reach out to Brad and say hello. Maybe mention that I was going to bring the girls to the picnic. I even started typing a message but realized that it would send the wrong message. I had already told him it wouldn't work, so why tease the man?

I plugged my phone in to charge and rolled over to sleep. As I closed my eyes, I imagined Brad next to me, his arms wrapped tightly around me as I drifted off. I was so tired and lost in the dream that I never even felt the tear slip from my eye as I fell into a deep sleep.

# CHAPTER TWENTY-FOUR

## BRADLEY

*I*t was the Saturday before Memorial Day, and I was sitting outside on the back porch sipping my coffee. Like I had been doing all week, I was dwelling over what might happen at my parents' house on Monday.

Kayley had shared that Nolan had driven to New York last night after work and was coming back today with the girls. I wished that I could meet them today and see their faces when they stepped into their new home—but no.

Hell, I wished that I knew what the inside of their new home looked like now. I was pretty sure that after several weeks, it would be completely different. The kitchen was complete, and Kayley said it was beautiful, plus the stone was up in the entry-way, the porch replaced, and most of the painting completed.

Kayley also told me that the furniture would be arriving in three weeks, and that's probably when the girls would move down. With everyone helping her, she'd gotten the project done in record time. Not that she didn't have other things that needed work, but the house's bones had been repaired and replaced, and now she could take her time doing the little things.

I was also disappointed that I hadn't been able to build that swing and firepit in her backyard. That had been a project that I wanted to do. Maybe we could find a way to be friends, and she would allow me to do that for her. My gift to her and her girls. However, it would suck to build something that I wanted so much and not use it.

"Dad," Tonya said from the door.

"Yeah, sweetie. What's up?" She came out to the porch and sat on the glider beside me. I put my arm around her shoulders, and she cozied up to me. "You sleep alright?"

"Yeah, I did," she said around a yawn. She remained quiet for a moment, and then she glanced up at me. "I talked to Ms. Nickels last week at the soccer game."

"I didn't know you went to a soccer game."

"I did, with Michelle. She plays on the team."

I forgot about that, and Tonya had spent the night before with her. "I hope you said hello to Ms. Nickels."

"I did. We talked for a little while."

"What did you two talk about?" Tell me every single word. Tell me she still looks beautiful.

"You."

My brows popped, although she didn't see that. She had her head resting on my shoulder as she stared out over the backyard.

"Me, huh? Pretty boring subject if I say so myself."

She giggled. "No, it's not." She grew quiet again, and I wanted to beg her to tell me everything, but I remained silent and waited. Finally, she spoke again. "She told me that you guys are just friends."

"We are."

"I told her that you don't smile as much now. You were smiling a lot when you were helping her, but you're back to how you were before."

I frowned. My daughter was way too observant. "I'm sorry. I'll try harder to smile."

"If you were with her again, you'd smile."

"Yeah, well, that's complicated."

"She said that too."

"She did?"

"Yeah, and she told me about her daughters. She told me that Lauren couldn't play soccer because she has something wrong with her heart, but she told me she likes to do other things, like read and do puzzles like I do."

"You do enjoy those things."

She nodded against my shoulder. "Her other daughter has autism like Beth in my class."

"Well, similar to Beth. I think Emmy is more along the lines of having Asperger's syndrome, but it's similar."

She got quiet for a few seconds. "Is that why you aren't friends with Ms. Nickels anymore? Because her kids are sick?"

"What? No! Not at all. What makes you say that?"

She glanced at me and then away. "Because you were happy with her, and then you weren't. I thought maybe you found out about them and decided you didn't like that."

"Aw, honey. It's just the opposite." I kissed the top of her head. "Nolan doesn't want to burden me with kids who have medical conditions. She said it would put too much strain on you and Tyler and me."

"Why would it bother Tyler and me?"

"You know, when people get together who have children from other marriages, it's sometimes difficult for everyone to adjust. I think Nolan is concerned it would be too much for all of us."

"But it wouldn't, and you'd smile more."

I laughed slightly. "Yeah, I probably would smile more. You're going to get a chance to meet them on Monday."

"I am?"

"Yep, she's bringing them to the picnic."

"Cool! Maybe I'll bring a puzzle that we can do."

I grinned. "You're a cool kid, Tonya, but maybe we can find some other picnic kind of things to do."

"Can we do sparklers like we did last year?"

"We can do sparklers. I think Uncle Hunt already has some ready for you guys."

"Good. What else can we do?"

"Well, maybe you guys can play a few games. I'm not sure if she can play lawn darts, but maybe she can."

"Do you think she can play Frisbee? What about bocce ball?"

"Maybe. I'm not sure how Lauren is feeling right now or what her restrictions are, but that's a possibility. I do know that she can't run around a lot, or she's going to get tired. Her heart doesn't pump the blood properly, so if she gets too active, it can't keep up."

"What about the sprinkler? Do you think we could run through the sprinkler?"

"Maybe."

"We could play jacks, and I can bring some board games."

"That's a good idea. Grandma has a few too."

"What about her other daughter? Do you know what she likes to do?"

"No, that's a tough one. We might have to figure that out on Monday, but I'm going to need your help with something."

"What's that?"

"Can you keep an eye on your brother and make sure he doesn't say or do anything stupid to bother Emmy? I know you have a little experience with Beth, so maybe you can just make sure he gets it."

"Sure. Ms. Nickels said that they haven't been around horses, so I'm going to show them the horses. Maybe we could saddle them and let them take a ride around the paddock."

"That might be a great idea as long as they aren't afraid of the horses."

"I'll show them they have nothing to be afraid of."

I squeezed her to my side. "You're a good young lady." I kissed her head again.

"Do you think that you and Ms. Nickels might go out again?"

"Well, between you and me, I am hoping that after she sees that we aren't concerned about the kids and their medical conditions, that she might give me another chance."

"It would kind of be cool to have two more sisters."

"Let's not get our hopes up that high."

"I won't. I was just saying."

"Yeah, well, you need to go eat and get your brother up. I have to drop you off at Grandma's in a little while. I have to work for a couple of hours this morning since I'm taking Monday off."

"Alright." She kissed my cheek and then hustled inside.

I was amazed that my daughter was so on board with this and thankful that she was excited to meet Lauren while being willing to adjust what she usually would do at a picnic to make sure Lauren was comfortable.

Would Nolan be able to see that my children could accept hers as they were? I hoped so.

Monday, I was at my parents' early to help get things set up. I was both excited and nervous as hell, but I had high hopes that things would work out. It was going to be a huge event, as not only our family, but the Winstons would be here too, along with several other family friends. If everyone invited showed up, we'd have over fifty people.

Hunt and Henley were there also, and we set up tables and

put up two tents to give shade. It was going to be a beautiful day with temperatures in the mid-eighties with low humidity.

The ladies were in the kitchen putting together the salads and desserts, and when Wes arrived, he brought the beer. We put Tonya and Tyler in charge of stocking the four coolers on the back deck with beer, water, and soda.

By noon, the seating areas were ready, and Hunt and Ethan were on the back part of the property setting up the horseshoes for the adults. On the left side of the house, away from the driveway, was the kids' area. We had kid's horseshoes and bocce ball. Plus, I'd picked up a ladder ball game and a bean bag toss. Even the old sandbox was cleaned out, and new sand was added for the little ones that might come.

Dad also bought a new sprinkler and had that ready for later in the day when they were getting hot and cranky. A few adults might need that too.

There were two grills ready to go, and the plates and utensils were neatly organized on one of the side tables.

It was shortly after noon when the cars began to arrive. I waited nervously for Nolan to show up, and with each car, I found myself just a little bit more anxious. There were about twenty people present when I glanced up at the sound of my daughter's voice. She was at the corner of the house, and with her were Nolan and her daughters.

Nolan was introducing Tonya to them, and I drank her in. She wore another pair of cut-off shorts and a sporty tank top. Her arms and legs were already sun-kissed with a warm golden tan, and I wanted to taste every inch of them.

"Cool your jets," Wes said beside me softly.

I laughed. "I'm not going to jump the woman."

"Yeah, you might not do that, but your expression says otherwise. Say hello to her, and then move along. We are going to start grilling soon anyway."

I looked at Wes. "Since when did you become my relationship coach?"

Wes grinned at me. "Since you thought you were a magnum." He slapped me on the back and walked away with a laugh.

I was never going to live that down, and despite telling them that I never intended to buy the magnums, they wanted to believe otherwise. I shook my head and went about moving some things around the barbeque area as I worked up the courage to say hello.

"Dad!" I turned and found Tonya behind me, Nolan, Lauren, and Emmy close to her side. "This is Lauren and Emmy."

"Hi, ladies. Glad you could come to the picnic."

"Thanks," Lauren replied. She was a miniature of her mother. Although rather pale compared to her, but her bright-brown eyes sparkled up at me just like Nolan's had previously.

Emmy didn't say anything, but I hadn't expected her to. "Hi, Nolan."

"Hi, Brad."

I forced myself to smile politely and diverted my attention back to the girls. "Do you girls like your new house?"

Emmy nodded after a moment, and Lauren was grinning as she replied, "Yeah, it's great! My bedroom is so much bigger than my old one."

"I'm glad to hear that."

"Dad, I'm going to go show them Buttercup and Fellow, okay?"

"That's fine, but you should have an adult with you just in case there is a problem."

"Aunt Riley is in the barn right now."

"Okay, then you guys can go over and visit with the horses."

Tonya started to dart off, then turned around and glanced at me before saying to Lauren and Emmy, "Come on, let's walk over and see them."

As they walked away, pride filled my chest. Both Nolan and I observed the three of them as they made their way to the barn.

"You're alright with that?"

"Yeah, I'm fine."

I turned to her once they had disappeared inside. "It's good to see you again, Nolan. I'm glad you brought the girls. What did they think of the house?"

She smiled at me. "Lauren loves it. I think even Emmy likes it too, although she doesn't show much emotion over it. We were going to stay at Kayley's while they were here, but they both wanted to camp out in the house."

"I'm glad things are going well."

"They are." She turned to me. "Brad, I owe you an apology."

I put my hand on her shoulder and squeezed momentarily. "No, you don't, Nolan. You spoke from your heart, and I didn't respect or listen to that. It's me that owes you one. I hope that after today you can see for yourself that you might have been wrong about my kids and me. If you'll excuse me, I need to check on something. Enjoy the picnic."

I quickly brushed my lips over her cheek, but I didn't give her a chance to respond as I walked away and into the house to see if the meat was ready to go on the grill. As I reached for the platter, I found my hands shaking like a leaf. Please, let this work.

# CHAPTER TWENTY-FIVE

## NOLAN

*I* almost wept as I peeked in on my girls sleeping at my parents'. I had arrived much later than expected after getting a late start. I could have gotten up early Saturday morning and driven up, but then I would have had to turn around and drive back without sleep. Four hours wasn't that bad, but eight hours in one day was a lot.

Saturday morning, the girls woke me up, and I even got big hugs from Emmy, who rarely hugged me. After breakfast, we were on the road and arrived at the new house around two.

Lauren was super excited to see it all, and Emmy seemed a bit more enthused than normal. Inside, Lauren oohed and aahed over things, and Emmy counted. She counted the number of cabinets in the kitchen, and the number of handles, being a bit frustrated that there was an odd number, but then I pointed out the three handles on the fridge and told her that made it even.

Then she counted the electrical outlets in the downstairs of the house as we walked around. Lauren rolled her eyes as we went along, but it wasn't from annoyance. It was more from, well, here we go again.

Emmy counted the spindles of the railing on the way upstairs, and when she saw her room, she grew quiet. Emmy had gotten this room because it had two windows. One window would have caused stress, but two was an even number and okay with her. She looked all around, nodded, and then walked out to see Lauren's room, commenting on her only having one window. Lauren and I shared a conspiratorial smile, and I winked at her. I showed them the other two bedrooms upstairs, and their fancy bathroom, then finally my room.

Emmy stared at the tiles in my bathroom, and I could see her mind spinning. Maybe all of this was too much for her. I was about to call her out, but then she walked into the shower and touched one of the tiles. Slowly she went along the row of the wall, counting each similar tile. I was thankful that it was an even number.

"Okay, ladies, why don't we go back to your rooms and talk about where you want things to go when your furniture is delivered?"

Lauren pretty much didn't care, but I knew Emmy would need to know precisely where her things were going. It would make it easier to adjust to the change if she knew what to expect.

That night we had a picnic dinner on the back porch with Kayley and Cameron, and Becky came too. She was turning seventeen soon, and she was great with the girls. After dinner, they went into the yard and caught fireflies to put in a jar for a little while.

We were going to head back to Kayley's to sleep, but both girls said they wanted to stay here, so I let them sleep on my air mattress, and I used the mat again. I slept a little better that night, most likely because I was exhausted. However, it might have been because I had my girls beside me too.

On Sunday, we did some little projects around the house and went shopping for new comforters and sheets for their beds.

Emmy didn't have too much input, so Lauren and I picked out her stuff. Although, Emmy did pick out two fluffy accent pillows that had very soft material.

That night we ordered pizza and watched a movie on my laptop. While the girls watched it, I dwelled over what would happen the next day.

Kayley had said it would be a more extensive picnic than usual and that there would be more kids there. I hoped that none of the kids were mean, and Lauren didn't end up bored because she couldn't run around with them.

The following day, my stomach was in knots. Not only because the girls were going to meet a lot of new people, but because I knew I would see Brad for the first time since I'd walked away from him. Over the last several weeks, I had thought of him a lot.

I hoped that we would have a chance to talk today and that I could apologize. Maybe, if I had the courage, I could ask him if he wanted to have lunch sometime, or if the kids got along, maybe bring the kids over for dinner.

I had wondered more than once if I had been wrong to judge him and make the decision for him that he couldn't handle my life or my children. I knew I had been wrong, but I couldn't help that I was protective. Not only protecting my heart but his and all the children involved.

When we arrived, the butterflies in my stomach were acting like Mexican jumping beans. I could tell that both the girls were a little nervous, too—Lauren more so than Emmy. They were about to meet other kids who would be their peers, maybe even some that they would go to school with.

On the way here, Emmy had counted the light poles along the roadway. There was one hundred and sixty-three that we passed on the right side of the road by her count. Who would have thought there were so many?

I saw Brad off in the distance when we arrived and was surprised when Tonya ran up to us and welcomed us excitedly.

"I'm so glad you came! I'm Tonya. You must be Lauren. We are the same age." She turned to Emmy. "And you're Emmy, right?"

Emmy nodded, watching Tonya for a second before her gaze skittered off, and she started studying the backyard. I needed to find something for her to focus on before her anxiety took over.

"Come on. I'll introduce you to my dad and make sure we can go see the horses. Do you like horses?"

That caught Emmy's attention like nothing else. She loved animals of all kinds. One of her favorite things to do was go to the zoo or the aquarium. She could sit for hours watching fish swim.

Huh, maybe I should get her a fish tank, I thought randomly as we headed toward Brad, who was working around the grills.

It was great to see him again, even better than I had thought it would be, and I took the moment we were alone to apologize. Only he wanted to say he was sorry. After only a few words, he stepped away, leaving me to stare after him.

Had I ruined any chance with him?

Kayley came toward me, holding Riley's daughter, Corey, in one arm and two beers in her other hand. "You look like you could use one of these."

"That obvious, huh?"

"Don't mind him. He will come around."

I twisted off the cap and put it to my lips. "What makes you think I want him to come around?"

"No one is that blind." She grinned.

We chatted for a few moments, and I looked around, trying to find my girls. Brad was talking to Emmy near the horse paddock as she stood on the bottom rail of the fence and held her hand out for one of the horses.

The large animal approached her and took what was in her

hand, and Emmy began to pet the horse's nose. The horse leaned his massive head over the fence, and Emmy let loose a rare giggle and smile as he brushed up against her.

Tears came to my eyes, and I saw Brad laugh and say something to the horse. Emmy kept petting her, and the horse seemed to adore the attention. Oh, man. Now she will want a horse, and here I thought a fish tank would be a good idea.

Brad remained at her side until Tyler climbed up next to Emmy but on the horse's other side. The horse threw his head back and whinnied, and then Tyler laughed. I couldn't see Emmy's face, but I had a feeling that smile might still be there.

Tyler said something to Emmy, and then he jumped down and raced away. My daughter turned and watched him go, then hopped down and followed at a slower pace into the barn.

Brad glanced around, made eye contact with me, and waved me over. I didn't need a further invitation. Inside the barn, Emmy was sitting on a hay bale petting a cat. Scurrying around the base of the hay where Lauren and Tonya were sitting were four tiny kittens.

"Mom! Look at the kittens!" Lauren said excitedly.

"I want a kitten," Emmy stated in her flat voice.

"I don't know about that, Emmy."

Brad grinned at me and said softly as he leaned toward me, "Might be a good thing to have around, especially if you have any residual mice in the house."

I turned my head, and our faces were only a few inches apart. Oh, how I wanted to kiss that man. "It's a thought," I replied before I turned away to keep myself from doing what I wanted.

He chuckled and said, "I have to go cook."

After telling them to stay out of the horse pen, I left the kids in the barn and spent the next hour talking to different guests at the party.

Coral was there, and she introduced me to her sisters Cara

and Carmen. I quickly learned that Cara was a helicopter pilot for the medical team in this area, and Carmen was a child psychologist.

Carmen asked a few questions about Emmy and said that she could help me with any special programs I might need for her. That alone made today worth coming—almost.

The picnic was a blast, and everyone was having fun. From time to time, Brad and I wound up in the same conversation group, and we'd share a look. Once in a while, a touch, but then the other would walk away.

It was almost four in the afternoon when I tried to locate my kids again and found Emmy and Tyler on the far side of the fence for the horses. They were walking along the bottom rail from one section to the other, and suddenly Tonya appeared at my side.

"Nolan!" She grabbed my hand. "Something is wrong with Lauren."

I was on my feet and following her as she pulled me toward the barn. "What happened?"

"She was jumping off the hay bales, and suddenly she said she couldn't breathe."

I heard other feet behind me, but I didn't bother to see who they were. I raced into the barn to see Lauren on her side, wheezing and gray.

"Lauren!" I dropped to my knees, and someone else showed up on her other side almost immediately.

"What's going on, Lauren?" Wes asked, and I'd never been so thankful to have a doctor as a friend.

Lauren said her chest hurt and she was obviously struggling to breathe.

Behind me, I heard Cara talking to someone, and it sounded like she was calling for help. Henley arrived and beside him was a medical bag. I was pushed aside slightly as Cara, Wes, and

Henley provided aid to my daughter. Kayley stood at my side, holding me tightly.

Cara shoved her phone into her pocket. "Chopper is on its way."

"Chopper?" I squeaked.

Brad appeared at my side. "They will fly her to Summersville. That is where Wes works. It's the fastest way to get her the best treatment."

"Can't she go to the local hospital?"

Wes lifted his head. "No, she needs to go to Summersville. We'll take good care of her there, Nolan."

Suddenly, I thought of Emmy, and I turned to find her standing at the door to the barn. Tyler was on one side, and Tonya was on the other, and they were holding her hands, all of them wide-eyed and scared-looking.

Brad put his hand on my arm. "I got her." Before I could say anything else, Brad took long strides to the door and scooped Emmy into his arms as he escorted the other kids out of the barn.

I didn't have time to think as I turned back to Lauren to see they had already put an IV into her arm and an oxygen mask over her face. "Where did all that come from?" I asked stupidly.

"Henley is on call today, so he has his paramedic vehicle."

Thank god! A couple of minutes later, we heard the chopper approaching, and Wes scooped Lauren into his arms while Cara held the bag of fluids, and they headed out of the barn toward a field behind the horse pen as quickly as they could go.

Henley came to my side. "You can't go in the chopper, Nolan, but I'll get you there as quickly as I can."

"Thank you," I told him as I ran to Lauren's side when Wes and Cara paused to wait for the chopper to land. "Honey, I'm going to be at the hospital soon. Wes will take good care of you until we get there." I kissed her forehead.

She nodded, and then she seemed to go limp in his arms. Cara and Wesley shared a look and ran for the chopper. As the chopper door closed, I saw Wes pushing down on Lauren's chest, and I almost collapsed to my knees. The only thing that held me up was a pair of strong arms wrapping around my body.

# CHAPTER TWENTY-SIX

## BRADLEY

$\mathcal{T}$he picnic was in full swing, and everyone seemed to be having fun. The games on the side of the house were keeping the fourteen kids busy, and I saw Lauren laughing and talking with several of them. Emmy kept more to herself, but she would wander over to the other kids once in a while, play something, and then leave.

Tyler followed her around from time to time, and I learned that she enjoyed counting. Tyler said she liked to count all the posts on the paddock, and they took turns doing it as they went around and around.

I was damn proud of my kids for stepping up to the plate and making them feel comfortable. Since they did, the other kids accepted them too, and for that, I was even more grateful.

All that changed when Tonya screamed for Nolan to come and that Lauren was in trouble. I went to Nolan's side, wanting to be there for her, but then realizing that the kids needed me more than she did. I didn't even hesitate to pick Emmy up and move the kids along.

"Come on, guys, let's go inside and find some ice cream."

"Is Lauren okay?" Emmy asked as she looked over my shoulder.

"They are going to take good care of her. My brother, Wes, is a doctor, and he fixes kids, so he's going to take care of her."

*God, please let her be okay*, I silently prayed to myself as I took the kids to the house. My mother met me on the porch where I set Emmy down. "Emmy, you are going to stay here, okay? I have to help your mom."

"Come on, sweetheart," my mother said, and Riley showed up at her side. "Do you like ice cream?"

"I like stuffed animals," Emmy replied in a voice void of emotion.

"Stuffed animals?" Riley asked excitedly. "I think I can help with that."

I was already rushing back to the barn when I heard Riley's reply and was thankful for Riley's addiction to stuffed animals when she was growing up. Hopefully, that would keep Emmy calm until we got back.

I ran out toward the pasture where the chopper had landed and saw Nolan kiss her daughter. I also saw her daughter pass out, and I knew that something awful was happening. As they started to take off, Wes was doing compressions on Lauren, and I put my arms around Nolan just as her knees began to buckle.

"What's going on?" she asked. "Oh, my God! Was he doing CPR on her?"

Henley stepped in front of Nolan. "Come on, Nolan, let's get you in the car, and we'll get to the hospital."

"Was he doing CPR on Lauren?" she yelled, and Henley peered at me momentarily before he nodded.

"Yeah, I think he was."

"Come on, Nolan. Let's go." I turned her in my arms and led her back to the driveway. Roxanne was waiting beside Henley's SUV. I climbed into the back with Nolan as Roxanne took the front passenger seat, and Henley was on the road in seconds.

I saw him flip some switches, and then the siren went on as we hit the road. Beside me, Nolan was shaking, and I encouraged her to put her seat belt on and I did the same. We were too far apart for me to hold her, but I took her hand, and she strangled it as if she were holding on for dear life.

We were mostly quiet, the only sound the radio crackling with someone's voice every once in a while. After one such time, Henley glanced in the rearview mirror. "They are at the hospital."

"Is she alive?" Nolan asked.

Henley replied tersely, "I don't know that answer, Nolan. I only know that the chopper has touched down."

She pulled her hand from mine and covered her face as she began to cry. I unbuckled my belt and slid across the seat, wrapping my arms around her shoulders as she fell against my chest.

I stared at Henley in the mirror. His grave expression did not make me feel better. Roxanne had picked up her phone and was making a phone call. A moment later, I heard her asking about the status of Lauren after she explained who she was.

She nodded and said thank you before she hung up. "She's alive, Nolan."

Nolan sobbed louder, and the rest of us released a tense breath. I remained where I was for the duration of the ride. I had been to Summersville a thousand times, but I had never made it there as quickly as we did today. Thank God for the emergency medical vehicle.

Henley pulled up to the ambulance drop-off at the hospital so Nolan and I could get out. He said he'd park and come in. I had my hand on her back as we rushed through the doors and stopped at the window to check in.

They opened the doors to allow her back within a minute, but I stayed in the waiting room. I wasn't Lauren's father, and I didn't have any right to be at her side, but damn, did I want to be.

Henley and Roxanne joined me, and Henley said he'd find out what was going on. Roxanne and I took a seat in the corner.

"She's going to be okay, Brad." She rubbed my back as I leaned forward on my elbows.

I barely knew the young girl, but I cared about her. I also loved her mother, and I did not want to see Nolan lose her daughter.

"She has to be, Roxy."

"She will be."

Henley came back a few minutes later. "She's stable. It looks like she had an asthmatic attack because of playing on the hay. The low oxygen caused her heart to work harder."

"Did her heart stop?"

"It did, and they had to shock her in the chopper, but only once, and then they got her back."

I raked my hands over my head. "Jesus. Is Nolan alright?"

"Yeah, she's better now that she's at her side. Wes said it was touch and go for the flight, but she's more stable now, and they have her on a breathing treatment for her lungs. She'll probably be in the hospital for a couple of days."

"But she's going to be alright?"

"Wes said the worst is over, but they want to monitor her for a while."

"Okay, can I see Nolan?"

"I'll see if I can sneak you back there." Henley walked away. A few minutes later, Wes came out to the waiting room, and I stood. The minute he was within reach, I embraced him—never so thankful for him being a doctor.

"She's going to be alright."

"Thanks to you."

"Yeah, well, if Henley and Cara hadn't been there and we hadn't gotten oxygen on her as fast as we did and into the chopper, we might not have saved her."

"I don't know how to thank you."

"You don't have to. Let me bring you back so you can see Nolan. You can't stay back there, but I can let you see her for a few minutes."

"Thanks." I followed him into the working area of the emergency department and found them in one of the trauma rooms. Nolan was sitting at Lauren's side, holding her hand. Lauren had her eyes open, but she looked exhausted.

I touched Nolan's shoulder as Wes stepped away to give us privacy. "Are you okay?"

"Yeah, I am now. Did they tell you what happened?"

"Henley did, yes."

I turned my attention to Lauren. "You know when we invited you to the picnic, we wanted you to have fun, but not helicopter-level amount of fun."

Lauren smiled slightly, her eyes looking a bit brighter for a moment. I laid my hand on her leg and squeezed. "I'm glad you're okay, Lauren."

She nodded but didn't speak.

Nolan stood. "Honey, I need to speak to Brad for a moment. I'll be right back." Lauren nodded again and closed her eyes to rest.

We stepped out of the room and started walking back toward the waiting room. "I don't know how to thank your brothers for what they did."

"You don't have to, Nolan. I am glad they were there."

She lifted her weary face to me. "Where is Emmy?"

I cupped her cheek as we stopped by the door. "She's safe, and she's fine. My mom is watching her, and Riley was going to get her stuffed animals out for Emmy to play with."

"Oh, that will help keep her calm. I don't know what to do here."

"Don't worry about it. You stay with Lauren; I can take Emmy home with me. I think she will be comfortable with Tonya and Tyler there."

"I hate to ask you to do that."

I took the other side of her face in my hands and tilted her chin up. "Don't say another word. Emmy is safe, and we will make sure she is alright. You worry about Lauren and yourself."

She slipped her arms around my waist and laid her head on my chest. "Thank you, Brad. I don't know how I can repay you all for what you have done and are still doing."

I held her tightly, realizing that I might have been given a gift through this tragedy—a second chance with Nolan.

"We'll figure something out later. You should get back to Lauren. Is there anything you need?"

"I don't have my purse or my phone."

"I will have someone bring it out."

"I hate to ask anyone else to come out here."

"Don't think twice about it. You might think you know our family, but the Youngs live for helping others."

"I'm figuring that out."

"I'll have someone drive your car out here so that you have transportation."

"Okay, that would be good."

I lifted her chin and stared down into her scared eyes. "I'm here for you, Nolan. My entire family is here for you. I know you don't love me, but I love you. I would do anything for you or your girls." I leaned forward and kissed her tenderly before I stepped away and went back to the waiting room.

The last thing I wanted from her was a declaration of love. She had way too much going on right now, and I wasn't going to add to her stress. I had told her how I felt because I wanted her to know how much I cared and that she was not alone in this.

What Nolan did with that was up to her, but I was in no hurry to push it. We had plenty of time to figure things out.

# CHAPTER TWENTY-SEVEN

## NOLAN

*I* had never been so scared—or felt so guilty.

Why had I thought bringing Lauren to the picnic would be a good idea? Why hadn't I left them at my mom's this weekend and followed the original plan that we had? If I had done that, Lauren wouldn't be fighting for her life.

Finding out on the way there that Lauren was alive helped ease some fear, but not the guilt. I wasn't one to fall apart, but I did anyway. I was glad that Brad was there with me. If there was anyone I wanted beside me, it was him right now, but what about Emmy?

I worried about her almost as much as Lauren on the way, but I knew that Kayley would make sure she was okay. She was safe. While she might get upset or throw a tantrum, it was Lauren's life that hung in the balance, not Emmy's.

I couldn't get to her side fast enough at the hospital, and I found Wes sitting at her side talking softly. Lauren was awake, and she looked relieved that I was there. I forced myself not to fall apart again, but I couldn't help the few tears that leaked out.

"We think that the hay might have caused an asthma attack.

Her lungs were pretty closed, and that put a strain on Lauren's heart."

"What happened in the helicopter?"

I was thankful that he was so straightforward. "Her heart stopped, but we shocked her once and started it again. Then we were able to get medicine in her to help open her airways. She's taking a breathing treatment right now. That's what that is." He pointed at a different mask she was wearing.

"Is she going to be alright, Wes?"

"She is. I want her to stay for at least a day, if not two, so we can monitor her. I already put a call in to a friend of mine. He specializes in pediatric coronary issues, and we've already requested her medical files from New York."

I startled back. "You did?"

"Yeah, Kayley sent me the information, so we called up there and spoke to the emergency service. Her cardiologist called me back, and I explained what happened. He is going to send all her files over this afternoon."

"I don't know how to thank you, Wes. If you hadn't been there—"

He stood and came around the bed. "Don't think about that, Nolan. Lauren is going to be okay now. I'm glad that I was there, as are Cara and Henley."

I hugged him, and he held me tightly as Henley stepped into the room. I focused on Lauren as they talked, and then they both excused themselves.

When Brad arrived, I wanted to fall into his arms, but I didn't. Not until we were down the hallway. I held him, taking solace in his strong arms and his soft voice.

I expressed my concern over Emmy, but he assured me that she would be fine, and he would make sure of that. It wasn't like I had a choice. I needed to be here with Lauren.

Brad took my face in his hands. "I'm here for you, Nolan. My entire family is here for you. I know you don't love me, but I love you. I would do anything for you or your girls."

His kiss held a promise that I couldn't think of now. I would save those thoughts for another day, but as I returned to my daughter's bedside, I felt calmer than I had since this episode transpired.

As I sat with her, she drifted in and out of sleep, and I realized that I wasn't alone—not anymore. Kayley had been my friend for a while, but now I had all of the Young family. I would never be able to thank Wes, Henley, or Cara enough for their quick thinking and their training. I was in their debt.

It was over an hour later when Cameron slipped into the room. They were getting ready to move her upstairs to a room, and he hugged me tightly and gave me my purse and phone. He also told me where my car was, not that I planned on going anywhere anytime soon. In his other hand was a small bag with a change of clothes.

"Kayley thought you might get cold sitting here all night."

"Thank you, and tell Kayley and everyone else thank you."

"Kayley wants you to call her. She wants to do a video chat with Emmy."

"How is she?"

Cam chuckled. "She is just fine. Wait till you see what she's up to."

I gave him a concerned look. "Do I want to know?"

"Just video chat Kay." He winked, kissed my cheek, waved to Lauren, and was gone.

I made sure it was okay to do a video chat in the emergency department, and then I called Kayley.

"Hey," she said on answering. "How is Lauren?"

I shifted the camera so she could see her sitting up and eating pudding. Lauren grinned. "Hi, Aunt Kayley."

"Hey, sweetie. You gave us quite a scare."

"Sorry for ruining the picnic."

"You didn't ruin it; you just added some unnecessary excitement."

We all chuckled. "How is Emmy?"

Kayley smirked. "Let me show you. I think that will answer your question."

"Emmy, your mom is on the phone."

She lifted her head as the camera shifted to her. Around her was an array of colorful stuffed animals.

"Mom, Riley has one hundred and seventy-two Beanie Babies!" Her eyes were wide. "I counted them four times. Do you want me to count them for you?"

"One hundred and seventy-two? Wow! How about you count them for me later?"

"Okay." She looked away, then back at the screen. "Where is Lauren?"

"Right here." I turned the camera to focus on Lauren.

"Hey, Emmy."

"You went in a helicopter."

"I did," she replied.

"Was it fun?"

Lauren laughed slightly. "Yeah, it was fun." In truth, Lauren didn't remember it, but Emmy wouldn't understand that answer.

They talked about the stuffed animals for a moment, and then Emmy said she had to count them again, and Kayley was back on the screen.

"I told you she was fine."

"Where did all those come from?"

"Riley was addicted when she was younger. She told Emmy she could watch over them while she was visiting."

"Well, thank Riley for me."

"I'm going to bring them home with me tonight so that she has them with her."

"I'm so sorry—"

Kayley gave me a stern look. "Don't you dare. You hang with Lauren, and we got Emmy. There is an army of people here who will look after her."

"Thank you and thank your parents and everyone else."

"You got it. Kiss Lauren for me. I'll talk to you later."

Wes came to see me right before they moved her and said that everyone was heading back now, but he would be out to see her in the morning. He hugged me again, and I told him to thank everyone again—like I hadn't already said it enough. I could honestly never say it enough.

An hour later, Lauren was in her room, and I had changed clothes. Lauren was resting, and I lay back in her side chair and closed my eyes. The entire scene played over in my mind a dozen times, and I was more thankful each time for the outcome.

Late that evening, I got a text message from Brad. When I opened it, I saw a picture of Emmy lying in the middle of my air mattress. Lined up all along the edge of the bed were the stuffed animals. I laughed as a second picture downloaded, and I saw Tyler and Tonya sleeping on a mattress beside Emmy.

I glanced at Lauren to see her sleeping soundly. I slipped out of her room and down to the lounge at the end of the hall where I called him.

"I didn't expect you all to be at my house. I thought she was going home with Kayley."

"Well, Emmy decided that she needed to sleep here. So, me and the kids are having a sleepover too."

"I appreciate you doing that."

"You're welcome." He paused. "Your house looks fantastic. Especially that kitchen. I didn't realize that you changed the cabinets."

"Yeah, after some long thought, I realized you were right. The ones I had picked out were a bit too modern. I love the more rustic look."

"It's beautiful, so is everything else. Your floors are fantastic."

"Thank you. They turned out even better than I could have hoped. There is still a lot more to do, but it's coming along."

"Much faster than you anticipated."

"Yeah."

"How is Lauren?"

"She's doing much better. If she is this strong tomorrow, they might let her go home."

"That's great."

"Yeah, except I don't have a bed for her, and I don't think I can take her back to my parents. I'm not ready to let her out of my sight."

"I can understand that. What if I found a bed you could borrow until your furniture was available?"

"That might work."

"Alright, let me see what I can do."

"Brad." I sighed.

"Don't, Nolan. I know you appreciate it, and you don't need to say anything else right now. Just say thank you."

"Thank you."

"You're welcome. Now I know you won't get much rest but try to get some. The kids were exhausted and crashed within seconds of lying down. They will be fine."

"Where are you sleeping?"

"Hunt brought me a cot from the firehouse. There was no way I was sleeping on that thin mat you have been lying on. My god, I wouldn't be able to get off the floor in the morning."

I laughed, and it felt so good. "I missed you." The words fell from my lips without prompting.

"I have missed you too, Nolan. Now get some rest. I'll see you tomorrow."

"Night, Brad."

"Night, Nolan."

I looked at the pictures again, and as I walked back down the hallway, I received another one. This one was of a lone cot sitting in Lauren's room down the hallway.

I typed back. *It looks harder than the mat!*

*It might be. I'll let you know in the morning.*

As I curled in the chair beside Lauren's bed, I closed my eyes and thought back on my time with Brad instead of the events of the day.

I think I had been very wrong about Brad, and maybe I needed to find a way to make it up to him. Perhaps we could make it work after all.

As I sat there, I tried to find the best way to show him that I was sorry and that I had been wrong. Finally, an idea came to mind, and I found myself collecting my cellphone from my lap to reach out to someone for some help.

# CHAPTER TWENTY-EIGHT

## BRADLEY

*B*ack at the house, Kayley asked how things had gone. We explained to everyone all the details, stating that Lauren would be alright, and Nolan was with her for the night.

There were still quite a few people at the party, and I grabbed a beer and dropped into a seat. Well, that hadn't been the kind of excitement that we wanted.

Tonya was on the side of the house playing soccer with some of the other kids. It was the first time that I had seen her actively playing. Usually, if kids started playing soccer, she'd stand on the sidelines and watch. Now, she was running back and forth and trying to steal the ball from the other kids.

Tyler had been playing, but he was taking a break, and now he was on the porch with Emmy. She sat on her knees, crawling around as she talked about and to the soft critters. They were now all lined up along the porch railing spindles from the back porch along the side and into the front. Whatever made her happy and kept her relaxed was fine with me.

Emmy looked up at Tyler, and they talked for a minute. Then he ran down the porch and started to pick something up but stopped and instead pointed at it. Emmy went to him and picked up the brown Beanie and handed it to him. He grinned at her and then raced away. Emmy disappeared for a moment around the front and then came back and set another critter in its place.

I drank from the beer as a few friends came to sit with me, and Riley squeezed my shoulder, winking at me as I looked back at her as she passed.

The next few hours were uneventful, and I wondered on and off how Nolan and Lauren were but didn't feel that I should reach out. Wes told me as he got ready to leave that he had just spoken to the hospital and Lauren was doing better than expected.

Kayley was on the back porch, talking to Emmy about something, and Emmy looked angry. "What's going on, Emmy?"

"I don't want to go to Aunt Kayley's. I want to go home."

"Well, your mom isn't there."

She lifted her gaze as Tonya and Tyler came to my side and replied, "But I want to go home."

Tonya turned to me. "Dad, how about we have a sleepover at Nolan's house tonight? Emmy could sleep in her home, and we could have a fun overnight."

"You have school tomorrow."

"So. It will be fun."

Emmy wasn't looking at us, but I knew she was listening as she kneeled on the porch.

"Emmy, would it be okay if we stay at your house too? Could Tyler, Tonya, and I sleep at your house with you?"

Emmy nodded quickly and asked. "Can I bring the babies?"

"You mean the stuffed animals?"

My mother was behind me and stepped in. "Emmy, you can take those home with you and keep them until your things arrive from the movers. Okay?"

"Okay."

"Alright, then let's put them all back into the bucket so you can take them home."

"Tyler, why don't you help her put them in the bucket."

"No!" Emmy said forcefully. "He won't do it right. I will do it. They have to be right."

Tyler pursed his lips and frowned, but then as if a light went off in his head, he grinned. "Emmy, how about I hand them to you one at a time, and you put them in the bucket the right way?"

She thought about that for a second as she shifted from foot to foot. "Okay."

I patted Tyler's shoulder. "Thank you, Ty."

"Sure, Dad."

I went to help clean up a few other things while they tackled that and put Tonya in charge of putting away the games and toys on the side of the house. Forty-five minutes later, we loaded into my truck and went toward my house.

Emmy didn't want to come into our house while we got our stuff, but she sat on the front porch swing with two Beanie Babies from the bucket. Fifteen minutes later, we were on our way to her house.

Kayley had given me the key to get in, and after I turned on the foyer light, I stood in awe. The entryway was incredible with the new stone wall, and the floor shone with a gloss that would last for years.

"Wow!" Tonya said as she looked around.

Emmy turned to Tyler. "Do you want to see where I sleep?"

"Sure," he replied, and Tonya and Tyler followed behind her up the stairs with their stuff. I carried the plastic container up the stairs and into Nolan's room where they had disappeared. An oversized air mattress was in the middle of the room.

The minute I set the container down, Emmy went to open it. "Wait, before you open this, you need to take a bath and put your pajamas on."

"A shower," she interjected.

"Okay, then a shower, but you need to do that before you get these out."

She stared at me for a moment and then frowned. "But Lauren isn't here to help me."

"I can help you," Tonya replied immediately.

"You sure, Tonya?"

"Yeah." She walked to the bathroom door. "Have you seen this shower? It's big enough for both of us. It even has two sprayers."

I walked to the door and scanned the interior. Wow. Milton had outdone himself in this room. It was incredible. The shower had been opened up, and you could walk in from the left or right. In the center was a piece of glass that went from top to bottom to keep the spray from going everywhere. Two large shower heads hung from the ceiling, and the entire area was done in shades of gray and white.

The toilet was raised higher, and the vanity now had two sinks that looked like large fancy bowls and had beautiful faucets. The lighting over the vanity was bright and warm, and there was a oversized framed mirror over the counter.

I could totally see myself using this.

"Alright, ladies, you two get a shower. Tyler, let's go out, and you can take one next."

"He can use the other bathroom," Emmy said flatly.

"Is that one working?" I asked, and she nodded, then turned her back on me and went to her suitcase.

"Alright, Ty, let's go look at the other bathroom."

On our way, I peeked into each room. I knew instantly which ones were taken by the girls as they had been painted. The other two were still the old dingy white.

While a little bigger, the bathroom was not as impressive as the other one, but it was still beautiful with beiges, browns, and creams in the tile of the shower. This one still had a bathtub, and the vanity had two sinks in here too, but not fancy ones.

I left Tyler there and went down to look at the first floor. I stood in the kitchen and was surprised to see that Nolan had opted for the cabinets I had suggested and not what she had initially chosen. It looked fantastic. Especially with the walls painted a warm honey color with a cocoa-brown trim. The color carried over into the family room, and the floors looked incredible with it all.

I ran my hands over the countertop; that was one thing I hadn't had any input on, but man, did I love the warm-tone granite piece she had chosen. I stood back, taking it all in and imagining Nolan hustling about to get a meal ready. I didn't mean to, but it was easy to add all four kids and me to that image.

A knock on the front door brought me out of my little fantasy, and I went to find Hunt at the front door. "What are you doing here?"

"I know Nolan doesn't have her furniture yet, so I brought you one of our extra cots. It's not great, but it's better than the hard floor, trust me."

"Thanks, man. I appreciate it."

"How are things going? Emmy doing alright?"

"Yeah, she and Tonya are taking a shower in Lauren's bathroom, and Tyler is in the other bathroom."

"Can I see the kitchen? Daniella said it was supposed to be awesome."

"Yeah, sure."

I showed him back, and he looked around the place, letting out a whistle of appreciation. "You know, I was never in this house, but I always imagined it was pretty nice inside."

"This place was a wreck when she first bought it. She had mice and snakes, and all the plumbing was rusted and corroded.

She had to have all that replaced and the electricity rewired, and we knocked this wall out here to open this up."

"You helped with the kitchen design, didn't you?"

I nodded. "Yeah. I did. It turned out better than I could have hoped for."

Hunt grinned at me. "Can you see yourself here?"

"What are you talking about?"

"Can you see yourself living here with her?"

"That's not an option, Huntley."

"But if it were, could you see it?"

"I'm not going to lie and say that I'm not interested in something permanent with Nolan, but I'm not going to move myself into her house."

"I didn't say that. I was just wondering if you could see yourself here with her and her kids."

I brushed a hand over my cheek and along my beard. "Yeah. I can. Before you got here, I was picturing all of us here in the kitchen."

"Then don't let go of that picture. Nolan is fantastic. I had a chance to talk to her today, and she's great. She also couldn't keep her eyes off you. No matter where you were, she knew, and she constantly turned to see if you had moved."

"No, she didn't."

"Yeah, man, she did."

Had she? I mean, I had found her looking at me a couple of times, but did she do it more often than I knew?

He slapped my arm. "The woman is into you, so don't back down too far."

"I won't."

We talked for a couple more minutes, and then I showed him out. In the foyer, I heard voices upstairs, and I climbed the steps and peered into the master bedroom.

Emmy was now in a nightgown and on her knees by the air

mattress. Very methodically, she was placing each stuffed animal in a line beside the bed.

"How is it going?" I asked, and Tonya smiled before she yawned.

"Good, Emmy is going to set up the Beanie Babies, and then we are going to read a book before bed."

"Do you want me to read?"

"No, Tonya."

I winked at Tonya as she grinned. "Okay, then Tonya, it is. I'll leave you all alone."

I set the cot that Hunt had brought over in one of the other bedrooms and added my sleeping bag. For a few minutes, I looked over the rest of the house, checking things to see the extent of the workmanship, and then I went back to check on the kids. They were sound asleep, and I took a couple of pics and sent them to Nolan.

I didn't expect her to call me, but I was glad that she did. She sounded much more relaxed than she had this afternoon, and I was happy to hear that Lauren was on the road to recovery.

As I lay down on the cot, I thought back on what I'd told her earlier today. I was in love with her. As much as I hadn't wanted to admit it to Hunt, I was all for moving this along.

Now, if only Nolan would accept the fact that we could make this work. I was pretty sure the kids and I proved that today.

# CHAPTER TWENTY-NINE

## NOLAN

*T*he following day, Lauren's color was better, and she seemed like her usual self. As she ate, I pondered a few things. I hadn't called her father last night, because quite frankly, he didn't care. I'd send him a text message later that she'd been in the hospital, but I knew him well enough to know he wouldn't want the details. He'd just want to know if she was okay. She was—now.

I still had to call my parents and let them know, but I didn't want to do that until I figured a few things out. One of those was to speak with Lauren and get her opinion on something.

"Lauren, what would you say to not going back to Grandma's?"

"What?"

"What if you stayed here and didn't go back."

"What about school?"

"You only have two weeks left. Maybe we can get your teachers to send you the work, and you can do it from here, then we can send it back for grading."

"Would they do that?"

"I think the better question is, would you want to do that?"

"I'd love to stay here, Mom. I love Grandma and Grandpa, but I love our new house, and I've already made some friends here." She frowned. "Although they might not like me as much now."

"Oh, don't you be silly. They are going to want to know all about your trip in the chopper."

"But I don't remember that."

"They don't know that. Maybe Wes can give you some details, and you can share them with kids who ask."

"Isn't that lying?"

"Hey, you were there, and you were in the chopper. They don't need to know that you were unconscious at the time."

She grinned. "Do you think the kids will think I'm weird?"

"Not at all."

There was a knock on the door behind us, and a man in dark-green scrubs and a white coat stepped in. "Hi, you must be Nolan and Lauren Nickels? I'm Joe Tesla. Wes referred Lauren to me as a cardiac patient."

"Doctor Tesla."

"You guys can call me Joe." He turned to Lauren. "How are you feeling today?"

"Pretty good," Lauren replied.

"Well, your cardiac monitor was strong all night, and there was nothing remarkable on it, so that's good. I'm going to listen to your heart and your lungs, and then I'm going to have a few tests run. Depending on the numbers, we'll see how long you need to stay."

"Great," Lauren said. "Hopefully, I can leave soon."

"I hope so too." He turned to me. "I received copies of all of her records last night and went over them. Wes said you were moving to Millerstown. I wasn't sure if you found a local pediatric cardiologist, but I'd like to offer my services."

"We haven't yet. I was trying to get our house ready; I hadn't started that search yet, but I would be glad to have you as her doctor. I trust Wes."

"He's a great doctor. I noticed a few things about her treatment that I think might be a little outdated. There is some newer technology and treatments out there now that have had some good promise."

"Really?"

"Yeah. After Lauren gets stronger, and when I see her in the office, we'll discuss some treatment options. I also have a patient who is almost fifteen who is undergoing a new treatment, and she is doing exceptionally well. I think she lives out in Millerstown too. I can reach out to her parents and see if I can pass her name over to you. Maybe you two can connect. I bet it would be nice to know someone who deals with similar issues."

Lauren's eyes sparkled. "Yes, it would."

Could we be so lucky to find a doctor that wanted to find a solution rather than just treat the problem? "Thank you, Dr. Tesla."

"It's Joe. Alright, let's have a listen, Lauren, and then I'll give you some other information."

After he left, both Lauren and I were in a better mood. He said that he wanted Lauren to stay one more night, just to be safe, but he had no reason to believe she wouldn't be going home tomorrow morning.

Lauren and I talked a little more about school, and she was excited to stay. Now, if I could just get her teachers on board. It wasn't like I couldn't help her with what she was learning. I was teaching the same grade she was in.

Now, Emmy was a different story. I felt that her teachers would pass her on to the next grade without completing another assignment. She got one hundreds on just about everything that she did, and missing a couple of studies at the end of the year would not hurt her. She might be stunted in her emotional and social growth, but she was not behind in her academic learning—in fact, she was almost two years ahead.

I called my mom after Lauren and I had made our decision. "Hey, Mom," I said after she answered.

"Hi, are you calling from the road?"

"Um, no, actually, I'm not. I'm calling from the hospital."

"The hospital? What's going on? Are you alright?"

I went on to explain what had happened and made sure she knew that Lauren was alright. "Mom, Lauren already has a new cardiologist here, and he wants to continue with her treatment. He said that they even have a few things that might help her."

"That's great, dear."

"I know. That's why I'm not going to bring the girls back. I'm going to get in touch with their teachers and work out a way for them to finish their studies here to move on to their next grades. The house is finished enough that we can comfortably move in. The furniture will be here in less than three weeks, and a friend of mine is working on getting me a couple of beds that we can borrow for the girls until theirs arrive."

"Are you sure you can finish the house with the girls there?"

"Yep. I'm much further along than I had expected, thanks to a lot of help from friends. The kitchen and bathrooms are done. The rest is much easier."

"Well, whatever you think is best, dear. We will miss them."

"I know, Mom, and they will miss you too, but after this event, I just need to have my girls with me. I need them close."

"That is understandable." For a few more minutes, we talked about details. After we hung up, I sat in the chair beside Lauren and realized I now had my girls again full-time. I'd have to find someone to watch them during the day while I worked for the next couple of weeks since they wouldn't be attending school.

It put thoughts of making things up with Brad kind of on the back burner, but maybe not. I hadn't asked Brad to step in and help, and yet he had. Of course, I had no idea how things had gone with Emmy last night, so today, Brad might be contemplating running for the hills.

I called him, and he answered on the second ring. "Morning, how is Lauren?"

"She's doing well. How is Emmy?"

"Great. She's at my mom's. The kids had school today, and I had to work, but my mother was happy to have her there. When I left, Emmy was putting the stuffed animals along the porch again."

"I'm so sorry this is causing so much of a burden to everyone."

"Nolan, it's not a burden. This is what our family does. My mother is happy to help, just like I am. Speaking of which, will we need to stay another night at your place?"

"Yeah, looks like Lauren is going to be here one more night."

"That's fine. I just needed to know if I needed more clothes for the kids. Guess who helped cook breakfast this morning?"

I chuckled. "Did Emmy help?"

"Yep, she has very explicit instructions for how to pour cereal."

I laughed. "That she does."

"Hey, I have a couple of beds being delivered today. The girls won't have to sleep on air mattresses anymore."

"That's great because they aren't going back to my parents' house."

"What?"

"I decided to keep them here." I explained my thoughts, and Brad thought it was a great idea.

"You know, I was kind of wondering how you'd be able to leave them again after this. I know that if that had been Tonya, I might not have been able to walk away."

"Yeah, that's kind of where my head was too." I paused.

"Brad, I know you don't want me to thank you again or apologize, but I have to do both."

"Why do you think that?"

"Well, first, you have stepped forward and helped me with so much. Not only you but your whole family. It is almost overwhelming the amount of support and love that you all have given me, and I know it's how your family is, but I need to thank all of them."

"You can do that eventually."

"Yeah, I plan on it, but I need to apologize to you."

"No, you don't."

"I do. I pushed you away and told you that I didn't want to be with anyone, but that was a lie. I was afraid to get involved with someone. I didn't want to be left again—especially if that person leaves my girls and me because of what we have to deal with daily. You have no idea what I went through when Rick left me for another woman and basically didn't want anything to do with our children because of their issues. I don't think that I could go through that again."

"Nolan, as much as I want to have this conversation with you, I don't think it's one to have over the phone."

"Maybe not, but I need to tell you what is on my mind, Brad. I kind of thought that all men would be like that. That's why I said that I only wanted to have sex with you. I was afraid that you would meet my girls and then run for the hills, or your kids would make fun of them."

"Nolan—"

I kept going. "But that's not what any of you did. You and your kids have been fantastic. I didn't give you or them enough credit, and for that, I am sorry."

He was quiet for a moment, and I wondered what he was thinking. "Brad, you still there?"

"Yeah," he said, his voice husky. "Sorry, I just wished that I was there so I could take you in my arms and kiss you."

"I wish you were too."

"Does this mean that you aren't going to push me away anymore? That you're going to let me date you properly and see how we can make this work?"

"Yeah, I think I would like that—no, I think I would love that."

"Good. Then once you get your girls situated, you and I are going to see where this goes."

"I think it might go pretty far."

"I sure as hell hope it does, Nolan. I really do."

A few minutes later, Brad and I got off the phone, and I felt like my life was finally going in the right direction. I was grinning as I went back to Lauren's room.

"You look happy," she said as I came in.

"I am. I'm going to have my girls back home with me, and we are going to finish our house together, and—"

"And what?"

I studied her for a moment. "What did you think of Brad when you met him?"

"I thought he was really nice, and even cuter in person. Tonya and Tyler are nice too."

"They are," I agreed. "Would you have a problem if I dated Brad?"

She shook her head. "Nope. As I said, he's pretty cute."

My phone binged with a notification, and I looked at it. "Oh, my god!" I said as my hand slammed over my lips.

"What's wrong?" Lauren said immediately, and I smiled at her to ease her sudden worry.

"Nothing is wrong. Look at this picture! Emmy is on a horse!" I turned the camera around. Brad's mom sent him a shot of Emmy on the horse, and he sent it to me.

"Look at her smiling!" Lauren said excitedly. "I don't think I have ever seen her smile so big."

"I know, right!"

"I am so jealous. She got to ride a horse before me."

"Yeah, well, you got a ride in a helicopter, and she didn't."

Lauren winced and then laughed. "Yeah, that is true."

As I stared at the picture of Emmy, I realized that I had made the right decision when I had decided to move. My girls would find happiness here, and I would find it as well.

# CHAPTER THIRTY

## BRADLEY

*I* knew that Lauren was home and resting, and I would pick up Emmy and bring her back to her mother after I got off work. Emmy had surprised us all with how well she did riding Buttercup. At the picnic, they had bonded instantly at the fence, but it wasn't until my mother was out mucking their stall that she saw a deeper connection.

Emmy had climbed through the fence and was petting Buttercup. She had her head resting against the big animal's shoulder as she talked to her and stroked her. Buttercup, who always loved attention, seemed even more drawn to Emmy than she typically was to other people. Anywhere Emmy went around the paddock, Buttercup followed.

After my mom cleaned the stall, she saddled Buttercup, and Buttercup had nuzzled Emmy like she wanted her to get on. My father put her into the saddle and gave a few instructions, and as if Emmy had been doing it for years, she took the reins and away they walked through the paddock.

My parents were spellbound as Emmy spoke to Buttercup in a way that she didn't talk to others. Unlike her normal voice when she spoke to people, her words held emotional infliction that brought my mother to tears.

There was no doubt that Emmy was now part of our family, and after my talk with Nolan the other day, I prayed that she would someday soon be part of it, too—officially.

Emmy was excited to see her sister and talked about the horse the whole way home. The instant we arrived, she was unbuckling her seat belt and rushing from the truck.

I caught up to her on the porch as Nolan opened the door, and Emmy stopped and gave her mom a tentative hug before she wanted to know where Lauren was.

Up the stairs Emmy rushed, and Nolan turned to me, shaking her head with a smile. "I'm chopped liver when it comes to her sister."

"She probably just needs to know she's home and safe."

Emmy appeared at the top of the stairs. "Brad, Lauren likes her bed."

"Glad to hear that," I called up to her before she disappeared again.

"Thank you for the beds—all of them. You didn't need to get me one too. I could have lived with sleeping on the air mattress a few more weeks."

"Yeah, but why should you? That's the bed you were sleeping on at Kay's place. The other two are from my parents' house."

"I appreciate that. Come on in for a moment." She held the door wider, and I stepped in. "Can I get you a beer?"

"I'd love one." I followed her into the kitchen, itching to touch her but not daring to.

"I see I have some pots, pans, dishes, glasses, and silverware now too."

"Yep, those are from Hunt. He didn't get rid of his stuff when he moved in with Daniella. He just boxed it up and put it in the basement for a future yard sale or someone who needed it. That should at least make it easier to cook now that the girls are here."

She handed me a beer and pulled out another for herself. "It will make it easier. Another thing I appreciate about you. You think of details to make life easier."

I smiled at her. "I am a man of detail."

She eyed me carefully. "I did pick up on that."

The two of us studied one another, and as if we'd both spoken, we set our beers down and stepped around the corner of the counter together. I took her face in my hands, staring down into those pretty brown eyes that had been part of my dreams.

Her lips parted, and she moistened her bottom one with the tip of her tongue as I moved closer. Her arms wrapped tightly around my back, and she brought herself closer as she went up on her toes to meet my lips.

As our tongues swept over one another, I felt like I had come home. Like this was where my heart was, and I had finally found it. I held Nolan tightly, loving the way our bodies fit together and savoring the taste of the beer on her tongue and aching deep in my gut as she whimpered slightly into my mouth.

I had never felt any of this with Cheryl. I had loved her, wanted her, but Nolan seemed to be so much more. It was almost like I needed her.

After a few moments, we pulled back and stared at one another. "I missed that," I said huskily.

"I missed that too. Man, did I miss that." She smiled up at me and then rested her head on my chest. "Come on, let's go sit on the back deck."

I followed her out and found that she had added two chairs and a glider to her back porch. She chose the glider, and I sat beside her and took her hand.

She looked at me. "Thank you for taking such good care of Emmy."

"You're welcome. She's a brilliant little girl."

"She is, and very headstrong at times."

"Yeah, I picked up on that, but I think we did pretty good getting around that."

"Tell me how you managed to do that. You didn't seem to know too much about spectrum kids before."

"Ah, well, Wes helped. He told me one day that if I wanted to be part of your life, I needed to prove to you that I could do it. He gave me a lot of information about the medical conditions that the girls had, and I did more research."

"You did?"

I nodded. "Yep, and I learned quite a bit. Tonya has been great with Emmy because she has experience with a girl in her class who has autism. I'm amazed at how well she does talking to her and avoiding issues. She's teaching Tyler a few things too."

"Well, I'm rather impressed with both your kids. I don't think any of the kids back in New York even tried to deal with Emmy. They just avoided her like she was a freak."

"She is far from that. It might have been her intelligence that they feared."

"Maybe."

"She's a lot like her mom."

"You think so?"

"Yeah, headstrong, smart, and beautiful."

She leaned toward me. "You might be biased."

"Yeah, why do you say that?"

"Because you love me," she said as she stared into my face.

I cocked my head slightly. "You're right. I am biased, and I do love you."

"I love you, too," she said softly.

"Do you, or are you just saying that because you feel thankful for all that I have done?"

She shook her head. "No. I do. I knew I was falling in love with you when I pushed you away. That's why I did. I didn't want to love you and then find out that you couldn't handle my kids. I didn't want you to leave me because my children needed extra attention."

I cupped my hand to her cheek. "I would never do that."

"I know that now, but before, I could only imagine you being like Rick. He bailed on us, and I couldn't imagine any man wanting to take these kinds of things on. But you did, and not just you, but your entire family. You have no idea how much that means to me."

"Everyone in my family cares about you and your girls. They would do anything for you or them."

"I know that now. I see that, and I am so thankful for that."

"Good."

For a few moments, we kissed again, and then she laid her head on my shoulder, and we glided back and forth in silence. The back door opened, and I expected Nolan to jump away, but she slowly lifted her head as Lauren and Emmy came out.

"Hey, Lauren, welcome home."

"Hi, Brad. Thanks, and thanks for the bed."

"You're welcome."

The girls sat with us for a few minutes, and Lauren wanted to know where Tonya was. I told her that maybe they could get together later in the week to visit.

Lauren got up to go back inside. "Emmy, come on. Let's leave Brad and Mom alone for a little while."

"Why?" Emmy asked as she got up and followed her sister.

"Because they want to be alone."

"Why?"

"Because they like each other." Their voices were getting further away but we could still hear them.

"Why?"

"Because they do. Stop asking why."

I chuckled as Nolan laid her head back on my shoulder. "You sure you want to be part of this crew?"

I kissed her brow. "Hey, my family has more quirks than yours does. You sure you want to be part of my crew?"

Her laughter filled the night, and I held her closer, feeling like, for the first time in a long time, I had finally found my happiness and a love that was just as incredible as the love that my siblings had found.

# EPILOGUE

## NOLAN

*I*t was the Fourth of July, and instead of celebrating at Patricia and David's place, we were celebrating at my house with a grand housewarming party.

For the most part, the interior of the house was finished for now. Our furniture was in, and we had unpacked all the boxes. I still didn't have a garage yet, but Brad promised to build one before winter.

The girls were doing incredible. Lauren and Tonya were fast friends, and Lauren had met a few others. There were a lot of board games played at my house and baking. It was Lauren's new pastime, and she was even talking about being a pastry chef when she grew up.

Emmy was thriving here. She loved to spend time outside, and Brad had even gotten her interested in building things. Right now, she was building birdhouses, and pretty soon, everyone on the block would have one, along with all the Youngs.

Emmy also loved to ride Buttercup and did so several times a week. Brad would go with her, riding Fellow, and they would leave the paddock and walk through the woods behind the house for hours. I asked him if he ever got bored, but he said he loved watching her interact with the horse and nature.

In return, I was coaching Tonya and Tyler on soccer, and they had begun to excel at it. I did not doubt that in the fall, they would shock everyone with how good they were. Both of them just needed a little bit of guidance.

I stood on my back porch and looked at everyone in the backyard. Brad had just finished the swings and firepit, and the fire crackled in the center of the group. The swings were filled with family members and friends, and my heart swelled as the kids laughed while they roasted marshmallows.

I went into the kitchen and dug around in the pantry for something I had hidden back there. With the long package in my arms, I returned to the porch. I headed purposely toward the swings where Brad was helping Emmy get the marshmallow off her stick and onto the graham cracker.

He glanced my way and did a double take as he saw what was in my arms. He quickly finished with Emmy and stood, setting his beer on a small shelf built into the support post.

"What is that?"

"A present," I told him.

"Who is it for?"

"You." I held my arms up, and he stared at the package. "What is this?"

"Open it," I told him as the kids rushed to my side. They knew what it was.

Brad took the package over to the table on the side, and I chewed my bottom lip nervously as everyone gathered around to see what it was. He gave me a questioning look before he began to tear open the package and then pulled out a long piece of wood.

There were eight of them, and as he turned the first one, he noticed something carved into the wood. His gaze flashed to mine. "Nolan?"

"I guess I need to explain a little bit."

"I understand what this is, but not why."

I came to stand in front of him. "I love you, I love your family, and so do my girls. You have helped me so much with my house and with my kids. I wanted to do something nice for yours. So, you built this incredible area back here, and these rocker panels will replace the top of each chair. Each couple in your family will have a swing here."

Brad blinked as a few people awwed in the background. "I love you, Nolan. You didn't have to do this."

"No, I didn't, but your family is my family, and I love them all."

Brad set the piece of wood down and glanced at Wes, who winked. He turned to me and went down on one knee as he reached into his pocket and pulled out a ring. My hands clapped together and came to rest against my lips as my eyes filled.

"If you love my family and me so much, why don't we make you an official part of the family. Nolan—" He looked past me, to Lauren and then toward Emmy. "Girls, I love you all. We love you all. Marry me, Nolan. Be my wife. Blend your family with mine."

"Yes!" I said instantly and then paused. "I mean, yes, as long as we are going to live here."

"You have yourself a deal." Brad slipped the ring over my finger and then stood so I could kiss him. Everyone congratulated us, and then Emmy came over to him. "I told you she'd say yes."

"Wait! You told Emmy?"

"I had to make sure it was alright with them."

I laughed as I hugged him tightly, and then David was pulling the rest of the swing panels out, and someone brought out a drill. A few minutes later, all the panels were attached, and the couples gravitated toward their swing.

There was a total of eight swings, one for each sibling and

one for Patricia and David. The last swing was for the kids. Each of their names was carved lovingly into the wood by me. Pete had come by to give me lessons on using the router. I was kind of addicted to it now.

I scanned the couples. Wes was holding baby Michael, and Charlotte was smiling softly toward Marisol who was still roasting marshmallows. The girl probably wouldn't sleep all night from all the sugar she had consumed tonight.

On the next swing were Riley and Ethan. I was glad that Ethan hadn't missed the picnic. Being a county detective, he got called away quite often on family events when he was needed. Corey bounced on Ethan's knee as Riley toyed with the hair at Ethan's neck, looking serene and happy.

The next swing held Huntley and Daniella, and Hunt was whispering something in her ear. Beside the swing lying watchful was Tigger, their dog. He wasn't watching Daniella, his gaze was locked on the marshmallows being roasted by the kids.

As I continued, my gaze landed on Henley and Roxanne. His arm was thrown over her shoulder, and she rested her head against him. He kissed her forehead and I saw his hand slip over her belly, pausing to cup it just so. His eyes lifted and locked with mine. He winked before he removed his hand and I smiled brightly at him. Looks like Henley and Roxanne might be announcing something soon.

Kayley and Cam were beside them holding hands. Kayley's belly was beginning to pop more now, and she ran slow circles over her belly. She had never looked more beautiful in my opinion than she did as she gazed at Cameron.

My eyes shifted to the last swing to the couple where it had all begun. Patricia and David sat holding hands, gliding back and forth, with pride and love shining brightly from their eyes. I caught Patricia's eye and she gave me a loving smile.

I was part of this family now, and I couldn't be happier.

As the sun went down, we watched the town fireworks

through the trees. The kids squealed and laughed as the adults sat around the firepit and stared in wonder at the sky, sharing kisses and tender looks with their loves.

I looked at the ring on my finger, the firelight sparkling off of it, and I knew that no matter what happened, I had found my forever. With Brad beside me, all four of the kids would have the love and support that they needed—and so would we.

*Thank you for reading the Loving a Young Series. I hope you had the opportunity to read all six stories: Wesley, Henley, Huntley, Riley, Kayley and Bradley. If you did enjoy it, you will be excited to know that there will be a spin-off series with the Winstons coming soon. Cara, Coral, Carmen, Candy, and Evan will share their stories as they finally find their forever loves, and you'll get some updates on the Young family that you have come to love. Look for the Sneak Peek to Cara at the end of this book.*

If you enjoyed Bradley, consider leaving a quick review! The best way too compliment an author is to leave a few words for them in a review.

Leave your review here: **Bradley**

The Loving a Young Series consists of six books involving the Young Siblings: Wesley, Henley, Huntley, Bradley, Riley and Kayley.

There will also be a spin-off of five more books with the Winston Family: Evan, Candy, Coral, Carmen and Cara.

**Wesley, Book 1**

Traumatized by events of her past, Charlotte Bennett is not a fan of strangers. When she sees a man touching her daughter at the park, she reacts without listening. It's only later when her daughter is rushed to the hospital that she realizes how wrong she had been.

Doctor Wesley Young only wanted to help the tender-aged girl he witnessed fall, but when her mother attacks him at the park, he's left stunned. When the little girl arrives later in the emergency department, he comes face to face with the mother who makes more of an impression on him than the cut she left on his face. Things heat up quick when Marisol is no longer his patient, but when things from the past are revealed, Wes isn't sure that Charlotte is the woman for him. Can Charlotte find a way to explain it all so that Wes will accept both her and her daughter before it's too late?

### Henley, Book 2

Being a wedding planner is hard, especially when someone is always trying to steal your business, and your family doesn't support you. However, Roxanne Novak is determined to keep her business afloat.
When Roxy's in a car accident hurrying to meet a potential bride, she's injured and scared, but paramedic Henley Young takes good care of her.

Henley loves his job and thrives on the adrenaline of helping people in need. Maybe that's why when he meets Roxy, he's inclined to help her with more than just medical care. Hooking her up with his older brother Wesley and his bride-to-be could be just what she needs. It might also be the start of something between Lee and the spunky little wedding planner.

When a position at a country club is offered to Roxy, she finds herself rethinking her entire business plan. Excited to start someplace new, Roxy and Henley begin making plans for the future. Just after she starts her new job, Roxy learns of Lee's past relationship, and everything she knew about him is questioned.

Can Roxy and Henley put the past to bed and move forward to

something that might be more than what both of them had ever hoped for?

## Huntley, Book 3

Daniella Knight works hard to create suspenseful and romantic tales, but after a violent interaction with a fan, she wants to hide from the world. When her house catches on fire, her and her protection dog, Tigger, are forced to rely on the help of strangers.

Huntley Young loves being in the thick of the action. Well, as long as that action has something to do with his job as a firefighter. When Huntley stops the homeowner from going back into the house, he has no clue, that he just placed himself firmly in the hero department.

As they get to know each other, Daniella's creative mind is always building on what is around her, and before she knows it, reality and fiction are hard to tell apart.

When danger strikes again, will Daniella be able to see what is right in front of her, or will her past trauma keep her safely inside her romantic fictional world?

## Riley, Book 4

Riley is always the life of the party, and it's Ethan that is there to pick her up and keep her together. He knows her almost as well as she knows herself, and he knows she will never love him as he does her.

Now Ethan wants more out of life and love, but Riley denies her feelings and insists they are just friends with benefits. When a training opportunity comes up that will get Ethan out of town for months, he jumps on it. It's the only way to get over Riley and move on.

With Ethan gone and a new guy in her life, Riley finds herself dealing with several emotional issues without the help of her best friend. A family emergency has Ethan feeling lost without Riley there to lean on, but he refuses to go to her and seeks solace with another.

Will Riley make the right choices, and finally, admit how she feels, or will she find herself alone and falling further down the rabbit hole.

### Kayley, Book 5

Independent Kayley Young is a real estate agent in New York and loves her life as a single woman. She's not one to get tied down, and she has no desire to have children.

Officer Cameron Sexton is new on the job, a veteran of the military, and proud of his dedication to the job. Unfortunately, he finds himself annoyed at his lackadaisical sergeant who should hang up his gun belt before getting someone hurt. When Cameron is dispatched to a burglary, he meets Kayley Young and is instantly attracted to her. Cameron has a feeling she reciprocates those feelings, except she's a little leery of the fact that he is ten years younger than her.

When Kayley's life starts taking a turn for the worse, she finds herself depending more on the attractive young man she has let into her bed for fun than she intended. Her original thought of enjoying the moment starts to last longer, but Kayley's not sure that dating a man ten years her junior is smart for the long haul. Especially with the rest of the changes that have happened in her life.

246

Can Kayley come to terms with the age difference, or will her family sway her away from the younger man?

**Bradley, Book 6**

Bradley Young is the eldest sibling of the Young family, and the only one who had previously been married. After losing his wife to cancer several years ago, he's used to caring for his two kids alone. The thought of dating is not something he's interested in, now with a busy construction business, and a family that always needs help.

Nolan Nickels needed a change, and with the help of her good friend, Kayley, she left New York and came to Millerstown to take a teaching position at the middle school. She has always been a huge tom boy and loves to fix things with her hands and play sports.

With a new house in her name, Nolan seeks out the perfect plan to get the house ready so she can bring her two daughters' home, but is her fixer-upper more than she bargained for? When Kayley finally gets Brad to stop by the house to check something, Brad finds himself more than intrigued with the spitfire, Nolan. Will he finally find the woman to spend his life with, or will she be put a halt on any type of future?

Ready for more Steamy Fun? Check out the Loving a Winston Series with a sneak peek into Chapter 1 of Cara on the next page!

# SNEAK PEEK - CARA, BOOK 1, LOVING A WINSTON SERIES

**Chapter 1 – Cara**

I kicked my booted feet onto the chair next to me as I flipped the page of the *Journal of Paramedic Practice* that I was reading. Every month when this came out, I devoured it from the front to the back. Maybe reading medical journals wasn't everyone's cup of tea, but it was mine.

I had become a paramedic when I enlisted in the military, but that wasn't all I had done when working for Uncle Sam. I had also learned to fly helicopters. Now, I worked as a flight medic for a local hospital, and from time to time, I changed seats and flew the bird too. There were eighteen of us that worked here, and five were exclusively pilots, six were paramedics, and the last six were registered nurses—then there was me. While I generally was sitting behind the pilot working on patients, occasionally, I took the controls if we were down someone. It was easier to call in another paramedic than it was a pilot.

Joe Taggart, Carl Vox, Jessie Turnbridge, Ronnie Sharp, and Stuart Muggles were the ones who mainly flew the ship. Sitting behind the controls was a different experience than sitting in the back. Up front, you had to make sure your mind was one hundred percent on flying. You couldn't think about what was going on in the back—at all. Too many lives were at stake, and it was up to you to keep them safe.

That's not to say that I didn't enjoy flying. I loved it. That's why I did some part-time private work for a rich guy who owned his chopper.

I thrived on the excitement of lifting it into the air and screaming through the sky. Much of that came from flying in a war zone, but occasionally, the risks were high enough here to bring that adrenaline to a bubbling high.

Yet, I preferred the heart-pounding adrenaline that coursed through my body as I worked in the tight space with limited equipment. Not that our bird wasn't stocked with everything that it could be—it was. The back had almost as many buttons and knobs as the cockpit. However, there was only so much you could fit into the space.

The chopper that we worked with was an EC145, a twin-engine that could reach 133 knots or slightly over 150 miles per hour. It was rare to push the limits that far, but there had been a time or two where we had bordered the boundaries for a patient.

I had never taken this ship over 110 knots, and that had made my adrenaline rush through my veins like a flame catching a line of gasoline. We won't talk about my speeds over-seas. Those were a little hair-raising at times and more often pushed to the mechanical birds' limits.

One patient that I had flown here at home at higher than usual speeds had been a young man who had been in a motor-cycle accident, and he had been holding on by a thread. He had still been alive when our team rolled him through the doors of the hospital and left him in the capable hands of the trauma bay staff.

Six months later, we received a letter from the family that

included a picture of their son. He was in a wheelchair and would never walk again, but he had a future, and that was because of our team. The family thanked us profusely, and I know that we were happy to hear the progress update.

It wasn't often that we heard from patients, but occasionally we did, and it was nice to learn of the outcome. There was nothing like giving it your all, then dropping a patient off and walking away. A little piece of you always wondered what happened after. We did get updates on whether a patient lived or died. That was only because of the paperwork that we needed to complete.

The door to the hangar opened, and Henley Young stepped through dressed in his paramedic uniform. While I went by air, he drove. I had known Henley since I was a young child as his family was very close to mine. Both the Young and Winston families had six children, although the Young family had four boys and two girls, and we had four girls and two boys—I was the oldest. One of my brothers, Evan, was married to Henley's sister, Riley.

The other difference between our families was that our mother, Rebecca, had passed away slightly over a year ago, and Henley and his siblings still had both of their parents.

I missed my mother every day, and while my father tried to step into that spot when needed, it wasn't the same. However, Patricia Young had opened her heart even further to shroud us with a mother's love when she felt we needed it.

"What brings you here, Henley?"

He shrugged. "Nothing much, just kicking around. Thought I'd see who was on duty today."

"Taggart, Rodriguez, and I are the lucky ones," I told him as he took a seat at the table with me, and I tossed my magazine to the surface. "You running solo?"

"Nah. No one is on the phone outside. How are things going?"

"Pretty good. How is Roxy?"

"She's good, busy as usual. Never knew that the wedding business was as hectic as it was."

I laughed. "Well, it is spring. Everyone wants to get married this time of year—except me. I'm never getting married."

He grinned. "Never say never, Cara." He opened his mouth to speak, but the radio he had set on the table called him. We both listened to the information about an accident involving multiple motorcycles versus an SUV.

He was on his feet as he responded that he was en route to the scene and then tossed back to me, "Get ready. I have a feeling I will see you there!"

He ran out the door, and I stood and stretched. If the accident was severe enough, he just might. I went into the office, standing at the threshold and skimming over Joe Taggart and Miguel Rodriguez, who were working on paperwork and watching a baseball game.

"We might get a call; EMS just got a multi-vehicle crash involving motorcycles."

Joe nodded. "Yeah, I heard it on the radio."

Miguel shook his head. "It's that time again for the bikes to be on the road. I hope they all update their organ donor status."

I chuckled, but it wasn't funny. However, it was a running joke. Most people in serious motorcycle accidents didn't survive, and if they did, they ended up like the seventeen-year-old boy who was now in a wheelchair.

Taggart stood. "I'm going out to the bird to do the preflight check. I got a feeling about this."

While he did that, I went to empty my bladder, and I was just coming out of the bathroom when our tones rang.

Taggart was already in his seat, and the first of the engines were turning on. My flight suit had been half on, and I pulled up the top and slipped my arms into the sleeves before I grabbed my helmet. Rodriguez and I were out the door in less than a minute, climbing in and securing our four-point belts as Taggart started preparing for takeoff.

I let my gaze skim over the equipment, ensuring it was all where it needed to be and secured properly.

Taggart asked us through our headsets if we were secure, and Rodriguez gave me a thumbs-up before I acknowledged Taggart. "Secure to lift."

A moment later, the chopper jerked as it left the ground. That jostling didn't bother me when I was behind the stick but sitting in the back, it was always a slight surprise.

As we flew, Taggart was in communication with the air traffic control local to us. Plus, the incident commander who would advise where the landing zone was located. It was a sunny afternoon with only a slight breeze, so the flight there was quick and easy.

The only information we received from dispatch was that the most severe patient was a white male, approximately forty-five, unconscious after striking a vehicle with his motorcycle. He also wasn't wearing a helmet.

Rodriguez looked at me and asked, "Tube or push?"

I grinned at him. "Why do you even ask? You know you hate to do the tube."

He smirked at me. "I'm trying to be a gentleman."

I laughed and shook my head as we circled the road from the sky. Rodriguez and I both stared out the window and down at the scene. I ignored the traffic that was backed up and instead searched the area where three bikes were lying on the ground, five to ten feet from each other. About twenty feet away was a mangled red SUV that was nose-first into the cement barrier, with a heavily buckled hood. I could just see the white airbag that had deployed inside the windshield as we shifted sideways and began to lower. The driver's side of the SUV was severely dented as if one of the bikes had run right into the side of it.

How did that happen if they were traveling the same way on

the highway? Had one of the cycles cut off the SUV, and it swerved? Or had something happened with the SUV?

Among the bikes and other wreckage cluttering the area, multiple cops, medics, and firefighters were moving around doing what they needed to do. Off to the side, several motorcycles lined the shoulder like metal soldiers preparing for battle. Men wearing black leather jackets, vests, jeans, and boots stood watching the scene.

Great. One of the biker clubs, please let it be a friendly one. Were there even friendly ones?

A few moments later, the skids were touching the ground, and as soon as we had the go-ahead, Rodriguez and I were moving. We grabbed our gear and rushed toward the ambulance, where one of the firemen was pointing.

There was another man on the ground, but a ground medic and an EMT were with him, and his injury appeared to be a broken leg.

A woman crying almost hysterically stood near the SUV, blood dripping down her chin from a bloody nose. An officer handed her gauze and glanced around like he hoped someone would rescue him from the female.

I pulled open the side door of the ambulance as Rodriguez went to the back. Henley was inside working on the man who was collared and silent.

"What do you have?" I asked Henley as I got seated at the head of the stretcher.

"He's been unconscious since I arrived." He glanced to his side, out the back door. "That guy said the SUV swerved and then lost control, turning sideways, and this guy didn't have a chance as he slammed into the side of it."

"No helmet?" I confirmed as I put mine to the side to put my gloves on and did a visual assessment of what I could see of the patient.

Henley chuckled. "Do you really think that's a question?"

I shook my head. Of course, it wasn't a question. Pennsylvania law said that riders didn't need to wear a helmet, and it would be a cold day in hell when a member of one of the biker gangs put one on their head.

The thick black vest covering the patient had a patch that said PRES on one side. Damn, it was the club's president, which could only mean trouble.

"Pupils are sluggish but responsive," Henley stated as I noticed the blood on the right side of his head. He continued giving me his other vitals. They were bad, but not horrible—yet.

"Was he conscious at all?" I asked.

Henley shifted sideways. "Hey, was he awake at all after the crash?"

I glanced up and then did a double take. The man Henley was talking to was holding his arm. His face was pale, and his dark-blue eyes were wide as he stared back at Henley.

"No, he flew back right after he struck the SUV, and his head bounced twice, I think." He shifted his gaze to me, and for a moment, the two of us stared at one another. In those two seconds, I saw several things in his eyes, including understanding which seemed odd.

"You saw his head bounce twice? Why were you looking at him?" I tore my gaze away from the man standing outside the ambulance and began to dig in my bag for the items I would need. I pulled out the tube and laryngoscope and set them on my lap as I did a quick assessment of his head laceration. With a gentle probe to the area, I felt the bone give slightly. That was where he bounced his skull, and it had fractured.

The man spoke, and I glanced up. "I was trying not to run him over. I turned my bike and laid it down so I wouldn't hit him." His voice was deep, husky, and held an emotional note that told me he was stressed.

Obviously, he was anxious. He had just witnessed the accident, and while he seemed to be injured, his buddy was by far worse off. He was probably considering that this could have been him—maybe that's what the understanding in his eyes had meant.

My gaze drifted over him momentarily, and I noted the scuff marks on the arm of his leather jacket. The same arm that he was holding. If he landed on it, he might have broken it, but he wasn't the one who needed my attention. I picked up the laryngoscope and prepared to intubate him.

"What's his name?" I asked him.

"Steve," he responded. "Steve Sheller."

I nodded and turned my attention back to Steve. I rubbed my knuckles over his sternum. "Steve! Steve, can you hear me?"

There was no response, and Henley commented that his pulse was accelerating. There wasn't time for any other life-saving in the field. It was time to do what we needed to and get Steve on the airship.

While Rodriguez was checking the IV line that Henley had already done, I prepared what I needed.

Rodriguez and I were working in tandem to do rapid sequence intubation, and after I told him I was ready, he began to administer the two drugs that would sedate and paralyze the patient.

Twenty-five seconds after receiving the Ketamine and Rocuronium, Steve stopped breathing on his own. "Go!" Rodriguez commanded.

I started to insert the tube. I struggled for a moment but finally got it fed down and past Steve's vocal cords. "I'm in." I clipped the tube holder in place and collected the bag valve mask that would breathe for him now that he couldn't do it independently. I compressed the bag, and Rodriguez watched the monitor beside him to confirm the tube was in the correct place. Once he received the ETCO2 report that carbon dioxide was indeed coming out. He gave me a thumbs-up.

"Let's rock," Rodriguez said as he put his helmet back on his head.

"And roll," I added as I did the same.

Two firemen helped us get the stretcher out of the ambulance, and after one last glance at the man holding his arm, I raced toward the helicopter with our patient.

### READY FOR MORE?

Cara, Book 1

Cara Winston has always been a bit of a rebel and an adrenaline junkie. As a helicopter pilot and paramedic, she relies on that to do her job.

When Cara and her team respond to a multi-vehicle accident involving motorcycles, she's expecting the worst. What she's not expecting is to find herself intrigued by the blue eyes of a man wearing motorcycle gang colors.

Ryan Vigilante rides the road, mostly on two wheels, not four. When several of his club end up in an accident on the highway, Ryan never expects to see a future in the eyes of the intense female paramedic. The only problem is, she's way out of his league, and he knows that getting involved with her could only put her in jeopardy.

With Cara's family trying to keep them apart and Ryan's club breaking the law, Cara finds herself more of a rebel than usual. Will things work out for Cara and Ryan, or will Cara's law enforcement brother, Ethan, find a way to put a stop to it for good?

# ABOUT THE AUTHOR

Stacy Eaton began her writing career in October of 2010. Stacy took an early retirement from law enforcement in 2016 after over fifteen years of service, with her last three in investigations and crime scene investigation.

Stacy resides in southeastern Pennsylvania with her husband, who works in law enforcement. She has two children, a daughter in college and a son serving in the United States Navy. She also has two grandchildren.

Stacy's favorite way to relax is to be with her family at Disney, or relaxing on the beach at Siesta Key in Florida. She loves the sun on her face, the sand between her toes, and the wind in her hair.

Be sure to visit www.stacyeaton.com for updates and more information on her books and sign up for all the latest on Stacy's Newsletter!

# ALSO BY STACY EATON

**Download a FREE Series Guide of books written by Stacy Eaton**
**ROMANCE TO GET YOUR BLOOD PUMPING**

This guide includes a listing of all of her current books and upcoming releases. It includes genre's, heat levels, series links to other series, and the first chapter of almost all of the books.

### Rise Again Warrior Series

Mission: Believe, Book 1 **

Mission: Accept, Book 2 **

Mission: Repair, Book 3 ***

Mission: Courage, Book 4

Mission: Gratitude, Book 5 (July 2022)

### Loving a Young Series

Wesley, Book 1

Henley, Book 2

Huntley, Book 3

Riley, Book 4

Kayley, Book 5

Bradley, Book 6

### The Loving a Winston Series

Cara

Evan

Candy

Coral

Carmen

**The Unexpected Series**

Unexpected Packages

Unexpected Arrivals

Unexpected Trouble

Unexpected Storms

Unexpected Desires

Unexpected Ties

**Paranormal Romance:**

*My Blood Runs Blue Series*

My Blood Runs Blue, Book 1**

The Pulse of Blue Blood, Book 2 (Short Story) **

Blue Blood for Life, Book 3 **

Mixing the Blue Blood, Book 4 **

Blue Bloods Final Destiny, Book 5 **

My Blood Runs Blue Series, Books 1-4 **

*The Return of Blue Blood Series:*

Kristin: Blue Blood Returns, Book 1 **

Hugh: Blue Blood Compelled, Book 2 **

Zander: Blue Blood Reborn, Book 3 **

Lena: Blue Blood Desired, Book 4

Reckoning, Blue Blood Finale, Book 5

Garda ~ Welcome to the Realm

### The Twisted Love Series

with Amy Manemann Co-Author

Love Lorn, Book 1 (Manemann)**

Love Torn, Book 2 (Eaton)**

Love Inked, Book 3

Love Drowned, Book 4

Love Carved, Book 5

Love Trapped, Book 6

Love Crossed, Book 7

Love Twisted, Book 8

Love Lies, Book 9 (Coming Soon)

### Domestic Violence – Crime - Suspense:

Whether I'll Live or Die**

Barbara's Plea

You're Not Alone**

### Romantic Suspense:

Liveon ~ No Evil **

Second Shield **

Distorted Loyalty**

Six Days of Memories **

Second Shield II: The Return **

### Contemporary Romance:

Tempt Me Too**

Finding the Strength

### Finding Love in Special Places:

*Stacy's Short Story Series*

Finding Love on Christmas Vacation

Finding Love on the Summer Surf

Finding Love with Dear Santa

Finding Love with a Champagne Toast

Finding Love on the High Seas

## Heart of the Family Series

Mistletoe & Cocoa Kisses, Book 1 **

Roses & Champagne Kisses, Book 2 **

Orchids & Hurricane Kisses, Book 3 **

Carnations & Hot Toddy Kisses, Book 4 **

## Heal Me Series

Cured, Book 1 **

Revived, Book 2

Mended, Book 3

Rescued, Book 4

The Heal Me Series, Books 1-4

## The Celebration Series

Tangled in Tinsel, Book 1 **

Tears to Cheers, Book 2 **

Heathens to Hearts, Book 3 **

Rainbows Bring Riches, Book 4 **

Sweet as Sugar, Book 5 ***

Making Mom Mad, Book 6 ***

Sparklers or Spankings, Book 7 ***

Raffles to Rattles, Book 8 ***

Flirting with Fireworks, Book 9 ***

Working under Wheels, Book 10 ***

Masquerading at Midnight, Book 11 ***

Blessings & Beans, Book 12 ***

Velvet & Vows, Book 13 ***

**The Celebration Series Box Sets:**

Part One: Books 1-5

Part Two: Books 6-9

Part Three: Books 10-13

**The Sometimes Series:**

Sometimes You Win, Book 1**

Sometimes You Lose, Book 2**

Sometimes You Play The Game, Book 3**

The Sometimes Series: Win, Lose & Play Set **

**Pleasure Your Fantasies Series**

Mistletoe Fantasies, Book 1 **

Whispered Fantasies, Book 2

Secret Fantasies, Book 3

** These books are also available on Audio

*** These books are coming to Audio soon

List Updated 11-28-21